The 'Bristol Study'

The Bristol Cancer Help Centre was founded in 1980 by Penny Brohn, herself a woman with breast cancer, Dr Alec Forbes, and Pat and Christopher Pilkington, to offer a range of complementary therapies, comprising a holistic programme for body, mind and spirit. From the start, it was stressed that the Bristol programme was to be used alongside orthodox cancer treatment, not considered as an 'alternative'.

Patients reported benefit from their visits, but many doctors remained sceptical of the value of such 'fringe' activities. The Centre was just as keen as the medical establishment to set up a research project to evaluate its work, and in 1985 a scientific study was funded jointly by the Cancer Research Campaign and the Imperial Cancer Research Fund to assess the Bristol programme in terms of both survival and quality of life.

Breast cancer patients were chosen for study as the largest single group attending the Centre, and the work was entrusted to researchers from the Institute of Cancer Research at the Royal Marsden Hospital. It was to last for five years. In September 1990, however, the researchers published in the *Lancet* the shocking results of only two years' s   These appeared to show that women with breast cancer   ell as having orthodox therapy w   and twice as likely to die once t   men receiving mainstream treat

These intrinsically impl   whole by the media, who had a field day.   were forgotten during the ensuing arguments between scientists, as a result of which the study was shown to be fatally flawed.

Many of the women fought back, refusing to accept the research results. In this book eleven of them tell their personal stories, illustrating what the Bristol Cancer Help Centre meant to them in their individual cancer journeys. A twelfth, the distinguished actress Sheila Hancock, contributes a foreword.

These women were the first group of patients to challenge the results of a study in which they had taken part. They represent a milestone in medical history.

Fighting Spirit
The stories of women in the Bristol breast cancer survey

Edited by Heather Goodare

**with a foreword by
Sheila Hancock** OBE

Scarlet Press

Published by Scarlet Press
5 Montague Road, London E8 2HN

Royalties on this book are being donated to
the Bristol Cancer Help Centre

British Library Cataloguing-in-Publication Data
A catalogue record for this book is available from the British Library

ISBN 1 85727 033 9

Designed and produced for Scarlet Press by
Chase Production Services, Chipping Norton, OX7 5QR
Typeset from authors' disks by
Stanford DTP Services, Milton Keynes
Printed in the EC by J.W. Arrowsmith Ltd, Bristol

This book is dedicated to
the memory of

Penny Birtwell, Frances Krivine, Sigyn Roberts
Hilary Scott, June Shaw and Joanna Treseder

with love

Acknowledgements

Without the support of several brave people, who encouraged the campaign of the Bristol Survey Support Group at a time when it was by no means politically correct, this story could not have been told. I am particularly indebted to Dr Richard Nicholson, Professor Margaret Stacey, Professor Karol Sikora, and Dr Richard Smith, who spoke up on our behalf. Dr Ann Johnson gave us invaluable advice on medical matters; David Hitchin and Kenneth Goodare helped with statistics. John Samson of Filmit Productions Ltd took the risk of devoting a whole programme to our story for Channel 4. Harry Lansdown worked hard on a subsequent programme in the *Taking Liberties* series for BBC 2. Jean Corston MP took up our cause in the House of Commons. Jean Robinson gave us support and advice.

Avis Lewallen of Scarlet Press has been all that a publisher should be: supportive and imaginative yet critical. I am indebted to my copy-editor Diana Russell for her careful attention to detail. Isla Bourke, co-founder of the Bristol Survey Support Group, made some helpful comments, as did also Michel Schiff. The *Evening Standard* generously allowed reproduction of the article by Dr Myles Harris on pp. 44–6.

Finally, I owe a debt to the women themselves who participated in the survey and have played a part in our campaign. All have contributed something, even if they did not feel able to write about their experiences. Several of their partners too have been a source of strength. As the American psychiatrist Professor Fawzy observed recently, 'The group has a magic of its own'. I thank all of them.

Heather Goodare

Contents

Foreword

Sheila Hancock, OBE

They say that everyone remembers where they were when they heard Kennedy had died. I am ashamed to say I don't. But I do remember where I was when I heard I had doubled my chances of dying of my breast cancer by going to the Bristol Cancer Help Centre. I was in hospital recovering from a gall-bladder operation. I watched, listened and read in disbelief as members of the medical profession leapt, with obvious relish, to condemn complementary/alternative medicine (they seldom knew the difference) and all its evil ways. It seemed as if this was the weapon to lance the pent-up boil of resentment festering against women who had strayed from the path of orthodoxy. For me, feeling particularly vulnerable in my hospital bed, their pronouncements were profoundly disturbing.

When I was diagnosed as having breast cancer I felt blind panic. The disease does not have a good press. Mostly I was very fortunate in my medical practitioners, although I too encountered thoughtless nurses who left me alone for ages in tiny cubicles, stripped to the waist and shaking with fear and cold, or gossiped to one another over my head while indifferently flattening my breast into a scary machine. I put it down to the 'You needn't think you are special – I'll show you who's important here' syndrome familiar to anyone in the public eye. However, reading of the appalling neglect and downright cruelty meted out to some of the women in this book, I realise I was incredibly lucky to encounter such relatively mild insensitivity, which did me no more harm than make me miserable.

My oncologist (a woman) is not only brilliant and *au fait* with all the latest information, but open to all except the most suspect suggestions of complementary treatment. Dowsing and metamorphic transformation didn't go down too well, I remember. However, she encouraged my week-long visit to Bristol and it proved a turning point for me. I entered the place convinced I was doomed to die a rather nasty death, and left comforted, relaxed and determined to change what was left of my life for the better.

I belong to a generation that was brought up to believe the doctor is always right, but my memory of that gentle week in Bristol convinced me that those who were condemning it as deadly had to be wrong. It was arrant nonsense.

I had been suspicious of the inadequacy of the forms I had been asked to fill in as a participant in the research study on the Centre (see Appendix IV), scribbling lots of extra comments to explain my inability to answer their questions by a tick in a box, which could not be an accurate answer. It all seemed highly unscientific to me. Indeed on the last form I filled in I was fairly rude about how meaningless I thought the questions to be. Never at any time was I approached to discuss my misgivings, and like the other women used for the research I have not received an adequate apology for my wasted time and effort and distress. Don't be silly, Sheila.

The whole thing has been an ugly episode for the research and medical establishment and has raised some questions about charity funding. It has highlighted the arrogance in certain quarters that leads to disregard of any clues that might be found in unexpected places, not least from the women themselves, which might throw some light on beating a disease that they have so far lamentably failed to conquer.

I am now privileged to be president of a charity (Action against Breast Cancer) where the research team is ready to consider more unorthodox paths, if only to disprove them with sound science. My involvement has made me more aware of the desperate lack of funding, particularly where no lucrative drug will be the end result. Also I find there is sometimes unproductive rivalry between research teams, and bewilderment in women patients who are given conflicting information – if they are told anything at all.

Researchers in the medical profession would do well to read this book. There may be some common threads worth investigating here. It will certainly demonstrate that, until a cure is found, treating patients with respect should be an essential requirement of palliative care. If necessary, for people to whom this does not come naturally, it should be a compulsory part of medical and nursing training. I refer to the dictionary definition of respect, i.e. 'To respect: – to avoid degrading or insulting or injuring or interfering with or interrupting, to treat with consideration.'

The respect I found at Bristol was invaluable for me. I am convinced it has contributed considerably to the efforts of my surgeon and oncologist to keep me alive for the last eight years. I am deeply grateful to the women in this book who fought back after the infamous research results were prematurely blazoned abroad. It is thanks to their tenacity and courage that the Bristol Centre has survived. I watched feebly on the sidelines as they took on the full weight of prejudice and pushed it back.

This book illustrates the personal battles these women were waging at the same time, and I am filled with awe that, in addition, they found the strength to do this on my and all other women's behalf.

January 1996

Introduction

Heather Goodare

'Now of course people who go to Bristol ... they've got fighting spirit, they're courageous, they're desperately keen, and understandably so, to move beyond the terrible loss of control.'
– Dr Jeffrey Tobias, *The Cancer Question*, BBC 2, 14 September 1990

When the paper entitled 'Survival of patients with breast cancer attending Bristol Cancer Help Centre' was published in the *Lancet* on 8 September 1990[1] the reaction of the women who had taken part in the study was first incredulity, and then profound anger. One of the most bizarre aspects of the situation was that doctors and academics were not only pronouncing on the gloomy survival chances of women who were in many cases very much alive; they were also making unscientific guesses about the *kind* of women they were. At last, in this book, some of these women are allowed to speak for themselves.

A brief résumé of events is necessary, for those readers to whom the story may be unfamiliar. Most medical research papers are published in medical journals and the participants never get to hear the results. This particular paper was an exception, because its purported findings were released to the press in a blaze of publicity.

In the study, which started in June 1986, 334 women with breast cancer who attended the Bristol Cancer Help Centre (BCHC) for complementary therapies (and also received orthodox medical attention) were compared with 461 women (the controls), who were given orthodox treatment at either the Royal Marsden Hospital or two district general hospitals in Sussex and Surrey. The study, which originally aimed to evaluate quality of life as well as survival, was planned to continue for five years, but in September 1990 interim results were published using only the data collected during the years 1986–8. (The Bristol women in the study

1

were still returning annual questionnaires to the research team, and thought the study was still in progress.) The results appeared to show that the women attending the Bristol Centre, in the words of the press release issued at the time, 'are likely to fare worse compared with controls'. It went on to say: 'The report found that the cancer was nearly three times as likely to threaten survival by spreading to other parts of the body in women attending the Bristol centre.'[2]

Although it was stated in the abstract for the study that 'The same information was obtained for the control group as for the BCHC group', this was in fact not so. One important difference between the Bristol 'cases' in the study and the 'controls' was that the cases were followed prospectively, from their first visit to Bristol, but the data for the controls were collected retrospectively, from cancer registries, and did not include any qualitative material: indeed the controls did not know that they were in the study, since their active participation was not required.[*] It was therefore not possible to collect data on, for instance, the smoking habits of the controls, or their use of complementary therapies.

The study was carried out by scientists employed by the Institute of Cancer Research. It was both funded and publicised by the two largest cancer charities, the Imperial Cancer Research Fund (ICRF) and the Cancer Research Campaign (CRC). A major press conference ensured that the findings of the study were widely broadcast on radio and television and reported in the national press. The result was that the women who had allowed their data to be used for the study were devastated, and the Bristol Centre itself suffered a blow from which it has still not fully recovered.

Immediately after publication the study was severely criticised by many statisticians and doctors, in letters to the *Lancet* and other journals, and the women themselves refused to accept its findings. They were not impressed by the letter from the authors published in the *Lancet* on 10 November 1990 which said, 'We regret that our paper has created the widespread impression that the BCHC regimen directly caused the differences that we observed in recurrence and survival.'[3] This letter was not given nearly such

---

[*] The protocol for the study was only submitted in May 1987 – a year after the work had started – to the Research Ethics Committee (REC) at Crawley Hospital, which supplied some of the controls. It was never submitted at all to the REC at the Royal Surrey County Hospital, which supplied further controls. (See Appendix III.)

wide publicity as the original study, which had done the damage. The women also pointed out that the researchers had not even made any use of the questionnaires that they had been filling in annually.[4] Some of them formed the Bristol Survey Support Group (BSSG), challenging not only the scientists who had done the work but also the cancer charities that had publicised it (had indeed trumpeted its results) without making sure that it was soundly based. They wrote a letter to the *Lancet* a year after the original paper was published, requesting its withdrawal,[5] and held their own press conference. In 1992 they made a television film for Channel 4, *Cancer Positive*,[6] in the series *Free for All*, featuring three of the contributors to this book (Rachel Charles, Vicki Harris and Anita Adams), and submitted a request to the Charity Commission to investigate the role played in the affair by the ICRF and CRC (see Appendix I).

In January 1994 the women's complaint was upheld by the Charity Commission (see Appendix II), which subsequently drew up new guidelines for the funding of medical research by charities. In June 1995 a series of scientific and medical research scandals prompted the Royal College of Physicians to make the first move towards a 'fraud squad' for the profession. In the same month the Bristol MP Jean Corston secured a debate in the House of Commons on an Early Day Motion (EDM) drawing attention to the plight of the Bristol Cancer Help Centre following the adverse publicity of the survey, and also calling for the establishment of a body equivalent to the General Medical Council to govern the field of misconduct in scientific research. This EDM secured wide support, and the signatures of 118 MPs in the parliamentary session ending 31 October 1995.

The Bristol story received further analysis in a BBC TV documentary *The Cancer War Story* in the series *Taking Liberties* on 23 May 1995,[7] in which two of the contributors to this book, Vicki Harris and Joan Ward, took part. At the time of writing, however, the original research paper has still not been fully retracted. (See Appendix III for a chronological list of events.)

May 1996 marks the ten-year survival (not necessarily since diagnosis, but since going to Bristol) of the first of the women to volunteer for the study. At this date the lives of these women become of great interest. If the original research project had continued, no important conclusions could have been drawn until now.

What kind of prognoses did these women have originally? How have they survived? What sort of women are they? Why did they choose to go to the Bristol Centre? What was their experience there? What impact did the publication of the study in which they took part have on them personally? Did it make them lose confidence in the Bristol programme, or make them even keener to follow it? What kind of lives do they lead now – if indeed they are still alive?

Each chapter in this book tells a unique story. It emerges that no easy generalisations can be made about 'Bristol women', except that as a group they have *not* 'fared worse'. In fact, some of them have far outlived their original prognoses. Some, however, have died, and four chapters give their stories: one in the woman's own words, one written by her husband, and two using material written by both partners.

This book does not aim to expose any further flaws in the study: enough has been written to make it clear that it is now discredited. It has long been obvious that the study is fatally flawed and its methodology inappropriate. The researchers were not comparing like with like: rather, they compared apples with oranges. What the book does aim to do is to put some flesh on the statistical bones, and to illustrate an aspect of the women's experience which was disregarded by the researchers (even though the declared intention was to study it): their quality of life.

So to return to our original question, what kind of women were they who went to Bristol? In the CRC/ICRF press release Professor Clair Chilvers (one of the *Lancet* authors) was quoted as saying: '... psychological factors have been shown in some studies to be important. It could be that Bristol attenders have a psychological response to their cancer that is different. We just don't know.'[9] The well-known cancer specialist Jeffrey Tobias on the other hand was sure that the women had 'fighting spirit'. In the television programme *The Cancer Question* already quoted he went on to say, 'if Penny Brohn isn't a classic fighting spirit patient, who on earth is?'

Dr Lesley Fallowfield also confidently asserted that women who go to Bristol 'are largely a self-selected group who are fighters' (reported in the *Evening Standard*, 14 January 1991).[10] I wrote to the *Standard* in reply:

As one of the 'cases' in the ill-fated Lancet survey on the Bristol Centre, I am tired of scientists making unscientific assumptions and hazarding guesses about us. Nobody has studied our psychological profiles or even knows why we went to Bristol in the first place; we were asked that only after the report was published.[11]

Penny Brohn herself protested that on diagnosis she felt 'a wimp' – helpless and hopeless. She thought many cancer patients felt like that, and said that she had set up the Centre 'for timid little wimps like me who had to learn [fighting spirit]'.[12] In my own case, I certainly went to Bristol to *learn* how to fight, after years spent in a wilderness of clinical depression.

The sad fact was that the researchers had collected data from the women through the questionnaires, which had given space for free comment and could well have shed light on this point. Sad, because the women had filled in those questionnaires in good faith, imagining that their comments would be given due weight and serious analysis. Not only was this qualitative material not reported on: the data on compliance with complementary therapies provided by the women were not reported on either. (It was like doing a drug trial without ensuring that the patients took the pills.) An example of a questionnaire is given as Appendix IV.

However, this book is not intended to be a contribution to the scientific debate. Its purpose is to give some of the women an opportunity to speak for themselves, to 'sing their own song' in Lawrence LeShan's apt phrase.[13] We have no means of knowing how representative they are, since they are quite obviously a self-selected group.

The women who volunteered, or were coaxed, into telling their stories in this book are just a few of the 334 who originally agreed to take part in the survey, on their first visit to the Bristol Cancer Help Centre. Since no qualitative data are available from the controls, we have no means of knowing whether they differed psychologically from the women who went to Bristol. Neither do we have any means of knowing how many of the Bristol women are still alive; the question we ask here is, if they *are* alive, what kind of life are they leading now?

Certainly many of the Bristol women had no wish to become involved in 'cancer politics', preferring rather to put the episode behind them, to concentrate on staying well, going back to work and so forth. We did not have access to a mailing list of women

in the study, so the forming of the Bristol Survey Support Group
was done through the self-help group network; it owes much to
the passion, enthusiasm and sheer hard graft of its first Secretary,
Isla Bourke, who by night worked as a BBC news typist and by day
pursued sleuth-like investigations into the ramifications of the
cancer world.

Only a handful of women wanted to join the BSSG: about 7 per
cent of the original 334. Few could attend meetings in London.
By January 1991, when the Group was formed and its aims
agreed, many would have died (the Bristol women as a group were
more ill than the controls, as the researchers admitted in their
Lancet letter of 10 November 1990). But remarkably, of the 23
women joining the Group, 17 (74 per cent) are still alive at the
time of writing.

It is tempting to generalise about themes running through
these stories. But what strikes me first about them is how *different*
they all are. What a remarkable bunch of women: how original,
how outstanding, how unusual, how diverse in background.
They certainly do not conform to the public image of Bristol
attenders as belonging to the brown-rice-and-sandals brigade. It
takes away from the uniqueness of each to be too anxious to draw
parallels. There are some uncommon stories here, such as Sigyn's,
starting in a woodcutter's cottage in Sweden; or Sumi's, with its
background of a Canadian internment camp.

Yet we can perceive connections too. Many researchers have
observed that people who develop cancer have often suffered from
broken relationships: first in childhood, and then again in adult
life.[14] These stories too reflect such a scenario: upheavals, ruptures,
heartbreaks, losses.

June was brought up very strictly by an uncle and aunt; I
myself was left in a boarding school at the age of five by my
missionary parents; Hilary, falsely accused of stealing at the age
of eleven, suffered from mental illness and, worse, inappropriate
treatment. Sumi's scarred childhood I have already touched on.

In adult life, Joan refers to two failed and childless marriages;
Rachel to the death of her adored brother; Geraldine to 'a failed
marriage and a failed relationship'; Joanna to a series of stressful
events culminating in the despair of infertility.

Some of the stories are incomplete in that they do not talk about
early life. This is because each contributor was given total freedom
to write about what was important to *her*. None has taken refuge
in a pseudonym for the purposes of this book, and this may

have inhibited them in some cases from revealing too-personal secrets. Their privacy must be respected.

Several have disturbing stories to tell about their medical treatment, which even at its best tends to concentrate on the tumour, paying little attention to the person: as Hilary says, 'I felt that I was treated as a carcinoma left breast and the rest of me was ignored.' At its worst, as in the case of Sigyn, it can be downright negligent. The ethics of research are shown up as dubious in Rachel's story of almost being entered into a clinical trial without her consent; while Vicki's experience of the private sector as compared with the NHS highlights some alarming issues of healthcare rationing.

Vicki's story also raises uncomfortable questions about cancer politics. Professor Karol Sikora has talked in a television programme (*The Cancer War Story*) about the 'cancer barons' who 'wouldn't want to have coming into their world alternative practitioners who were regarded as cranks', and Vicki asks, 'What are the big boys afraid of?' In the same TV programme Joan Ward also commented: 'Powerful people didn't obey the rules.'

Running through these stories is the message that women go to Bristol because their needs are not being met by the NHS: it is rare for them to be given appropriate information, partnership with clinicians in choice of treatments, or emotional support. Surgeons are felt to be inept at delivering bad news. A shining exception to the generally gloomy picture is the story of June, whose excellent orthodox treatment, together with the approach of the Bristol Centre and her own fighting spirit, gave her both long survival and joyous quality of life.

In the cases of these women, their primary treatment goes back ten years and more, but recent studies make it clear that we still have a very long way to go before we achieve an acceptable service for cancer patients in the UK.[15]

Emotional support is a key need: but there have been misunderstandings here. The pioneering work of Steven Greer and his colleagues at the Royal Marsden Hospital, who first identified 'fighting spirit' as a key element in survival of breast cancer patients,[16] has been perhaps misrepresented as advocating 'positive thinking' at all costs. What may be more important is to allow the patient's own authentic voice to be heard, even if she expresses negative feelings. As David Spiegel found,[17] expressing anger and despair and talking about death may actually be of therapeutic benefit. Joanna says:

yes, it is about ... acceptance and support. It is also about doubt, anger, guilt and despair. When I have been supported in recognising and expressing those feelings, I have at times experienced great joy and a deep sense of the fullness of life.

Joanna's perception of the importance of emotional issues led her to train as a counsellor, as did Sigyn and Rachel too. All three were also intensely interested in nutritional approaches, and Joanna and Sigyn went well beyond the recommendations of the BCHC to try the much more severe dietary regime of Max Gerson.[18] This approach always raises eyebrows among orthodox clinicians, but when chemotherapy only improves survival rates of breast cancer patients by a small margin,[19] and the Gerson approach has achieved remarkable recoveries among apparently hopeless cases,[20] we should stop talking about 'anecdotal evidence' and 'spontaneous remission' and start replicating the studies already done so that a reliable body of evidence can be built up and appropriate action taken.

Further familiar themes are those of recovery. There seems to be a pattern here of restoring harmony and connectedness: particularly moving is Sumi's account of her reunion with her brothers and sisters, survivors of the internment camp, after 50 years. Rachel, in spite of the early suspicion of secondary spread to the ribs, went on to find a new life and new relationships, and continues well.

The comparative youth of these women is also a striking phenomenon. As a group, the Bristol 'cases' were considerably younger than the controls, and there is clear evidence (denied by the researchers) that tumours tend to grow faster in younger women.[21] Sadly, among the younger women Joanna and Hilary have died, but Geraldine, Rachel, Vicki and Joan are still with us.

This book is being published at a time when the UK National Breast Cancer Coalition is making itself felt, and breast cancer patients are being patient no more.[22] The Bristol women were the first to challenge the results of a study in which they had taken part. In future the voices of women with experience of the disease must be heard. These stories illustrate the themes of the Coalition, which demands access for all to state-of-the-art treatment for breast cancer, including psychosocial support; increased government spending on research into issues of importance to women themselves (especially causes, prevention and quality of life); and for women to have an influential role in decisions on all breast cancer issues.

So what of 'fighting spirit'? Did these women possess fighting spirit before they went to Bristol, or did they acquire it there? The reader must judge. But one important point emerges from these stories. Several contributors were surprised and shocked that the Centre itself appeared not to 'fight back' when the ill-fated survey was published, and seemed on the contrary to lose confidence in its own philosophy. In Vicki's words:

> ... here was Bristol back-tracking on its methods and therapies. They were questioning themselves, something I never dreamed of doing. Bristol had taught us to have faith in ourselves and our abilities. Why were they so worried? I was angry that they had lost faith in themselves.

As Anita says, 'You see, Bristol taught us to fight back when the odds were against us – and that's exactly what we did.' The 'fighting spirit' of the Bristol Survey Support Group was perhaps more than even the Centre itself had bargained for. In 'fighting back' the 'Bristol women' have led the way. I am proud to be one of them.

Notes and References

1 Bagenal, F.S., Easton, D.F., Harris, E., Chilvers, C.E.D. and McElwain, T.J. 'Survival of patients with breast cancer attending Bristol Cancer Help Centre'. *Lancet* 1990; 336: 606–10.

2 Cancer Research Campaign and Imperial Cancer Research Fund (CRC/ICRF). 'Report on Alternative Cancer Therapy: press release embargoed until 00.01 hours, Friday 7 September 1990'. (The embargo was in fact broken by the *Evening Standard* on 5 September, followed immediately by radio and television.)

3 Chilvers, C.E.D., Easton, D.F., Bagenal, F.S., Harris, E. and McElwain, T.J. 'Bristol Cancer Help Centre'. *Lancet* 1990; 336: 1186–8.

4 Goodare, H. 'Bristol: a patient's view.' *Link-up* (newsletter of CancerLink) Winter 1990/91; 22: 8.

5 Bourke, I. and Goodare, H. 'Bristol Cancer Help Centre.' *Lancet* 1991 (Nov.); 338: 1401.

6 *Cancer Positive* by Isla Bourke and Heather Goodare, in the series *Free for All*, produced by Yasmin Anwar for Filmit Productions Ltd; Channel 4, 2 April 1992, repeated with an 'update' on 23 July 1992.

7   *The Cancer War Story*, in the series *Taking Liberties*, BBC 2, 23 May 1995, produced by John Farren.

8   *The Cancer Question*, BBC 2, 14 September 1990 (second of two programmes), *The Public Eye Debate*, produced by David Henshaw and Nigel Chapman.

9   CRC/ICRF. 'Report on Alternative Cancer Therapy' (see note 2).

10   McAfee, A. 'On the side of the fighters'. *Evening Standard* 14 January 1991, p. 22.

11   Goodare, H. 'Cancer guesses'. *Evening Standard* 19 January 1991, p. 19.

12   On *The Cancer Question*, BBC2, 14 September 1990.

13   LeShan, L. *Cancer as a Turning Point* 1989; Bath: Gateway, p. 36.

14   For a summary of the research in this field see Guex, P., *An Introduction to Psycho-oncology* trans. H Goodare 1993; London: Routledge. See also Maunsell, E., Brisson, J. and Deschênes, L. 'Psychological distress after initial treatment of breast cancer: assessment of potential risk factors'. *Cancer* 1992; 70 (1): 120–5; Chen, C.C., David, A.S., Nunnerley, H. et al. 'Adverse life events and breast cancer: case-control study'. *British Medical Journal* 1995; 311: 1527–30.

15   Fallowfield, L., Ford, S. and Lewis, S. 'No news is not good news: information preferences of patients with cancer'. *Psycho-oncology* 1995; 4: 197–202. See also: Audit Commission. *Communication with Patients in Hospital*, 1993, London: HMSO.

16   Greer, S., Morris, T. and Pettingale, K.W. 'Psychological response to breast cancer: effect on outcome'. *Lancet* 1979; ii: 785–7.

17   Spiegel, D. *Living beyond Limits: new hope and help for facing life-threatening illness* 1993; New York: Random House.

18   Gerson, M. *A Cancer Therapy: results of fifty cases*, 5th edn. 1990; Bonita, Calif.: Gerson Institute (first published 1958).

19   Early Breast Cancer Trialists' Collaborative Group. 'Systemic treatment of early breast cancer by hormonal, cytotoxic, or immune therapy'. *Lancet* 1992; 339: 1–15, 71–85.

20   Hildenbrand, G., Hildenbrand, L.C., Bradford, K. and Cavin, S.W. 'Five-year survival rates of melanoma patients treated by diet therapy after the manner of Gerson: a retrospective review'. *Alternative Therapies in Health and Medicine* 1995; 1 (4): 29–37.

21   See for example Falkson, G., Gelman, R.S. and Pretorius, F.J. 'Age as a prognostic factor in recurrent breast cancer'. *Journal of Clinical Oncology* 1986; 4 (5): 663–71. The BSSG submission to the Charity Commission listed 14 studies published before 1990 in which it was found that young age was an adverse prognostic factor. Subsequent studies have confirmed this finding, for example Rochefordière, A. de la, Asselain, B., Campana, F., *et al.*, 'Age as a prognostic factor in premenopausal breast carcinoma', *Lancet* 1993; 341: 1039–43.

22   Batt, S. *Patient No More: the politics of breast cancer*, 1995, London: Scarlet Press.

1 My World Upside Down

Anita Adams

Anita, aged 45 on diagnosis in 1987, runs a needlecraft shop in east London. She was featured in the television film *Cancer Positive* (1992). Happily married to Ken for 30 years, she has two grown-up children.

As I sit and reflect on the eighth anniversary of my world turning upside down it is sometimes difficult to realise it's me that it has happened to: I sometimes get this feeling of detachment, as if I'm an onlooker.

Ever since I had my children – Tony and Vanessa – I had suffered continuously from mastitis and lumpy breasts, and had been referred to a specialist in the mid-1970s, so as far as I am concerned I was a possible candidate for future problems. Unfortunately, they do not appear to keep an eye on you.

In July 1986 we were travelling to a wedding in Norfolk. My husband Ken was driving and I was just relaxing beside him. My hand brushed against my blouse – it was as if I had had an electric shock: I felt a lump the size of a *petit pois* in my left breast. I was too shocked to say a word to Ken. All through the wedding ceremony I was in a daze. As soon as we arrived at the reception I headed for the ladies' to double-check – yes, the lump was still there. The next day when we returned home, as I showered I examined myself – it had disappeared. For several days I continued to check, but there was no sign of it.

I decided to find out whether it was possible to have a mammogram done. Unfortunately, our local private hospital did not install a machine until May 1987, and I did not think I had grounds to go to my GP. He would have been sympathetic; but how do you explain a lump that has disappeared? I now realise it was probably the start of my troubles.

In January 1987, almost overnight, I developed rheumatoid arthritis in my hands and feet. My hands were so painful that for a couple of months I was unable to examine my breasts.

I jumped out of bed bright and early on Easter Saturday 1987, showered and then realised I had plenty of time to get ready for work. So I jumped back into bed, but got in on Ken's side. He put his arm across and then came the shock – he felt the lump in my left breast. It was the size of a broad bean. I leapt out of bed with a feeling of fear: facing that moment every woman prays will never come to her. Ken suggested I contact the doctor. I telephoned the surgery and the receptionist asked if it was urgent, as Saturdays were for urgent cases only. I replied 'No!' but inside my brain was screaming, 'Yes it's urgent, very urgent!' An appointment was made for the following Tuesday morning, and I decided to go to work as usual. Life had to go on as normal. Rhoda, my business partner and friend, felt as sick as I did when I told her. I think you go on autopilot.

Tuesday came, and thank goodness I have a doctor who sends you straight to the hospital if he has any doubts. No coming back in two months' time – as often happens to women in the same position. He telephoned the hospital straight away and luckily the surgeon had a clinic that day. When he inspected the lump he never said a word. There you are, waiting for encouraging news and trying to read his mind from his expression – or lack of it. But at least he looked like a man I could put my trust in. He said that I would have to come in, but that it did not mean that I would have to have a mastectomy, that it was not always necessary these days. In blind panic I said that if it saved my life I wasn't really bothered. When I saw him write DO NOT CANCEL on my notes I knew it was not good news.

I went into hospital on the Thursday, and Friday was op. day when a small contingent of us went down with suspect lumps. On Saturday morning my surgeon and his two young housemen came into our two-bedded ward. He walked over to the window – the furthest point from my bed – and began: 'Mrs Adams, we removed a tumour, but the good news is that your blood tests are clear.' I didn't hear the rest of his words; it was as if he was standing there with a gun shooting the words out. My room-mate was trying her hardest to explain it to me afterwards. No one was holding my hand, and neither was my husband told in advance, so when he came in to see me I found it hard to 'spill the beans'. In fact when I told one friend, the way I told her she thought I was OK. I was like a zombie. They kept me in until the following Tuesday, when a Sister from one of the other wards who had just started a part-time breast clinic could have a chat with me.

Unfortunately, she had to fit it in with her normal ward duties. But I was able to have a cry and then came to terms with the situation. I understand that now there is a team involved. So thankfully in eight years the treatment and care have improved greatly. I believe that a trained counsellor/nurse should be with the patient when she is told such shattering news, and that a support group should be available with all the relevant information.

The only other time I cried was when I went to be measured up for radiotherapy. You feel so alone as you lie there with that big machine hovering over you. You have to keep so still – and why is it that your nose always tickles at such a moment?

Two days before I was due to start my radiotherapy I was sitting in the car, stationary, while Ken got out to get some beers. As he stood waiting at the roadside, he was powerless to help as another car crashed into the back of ours. The force sent our dog from the back seat to the front. My neck felt as if it was coming away from my head. The driver asked if I was OK – all I could think of was, what sort of shock was it to my already battered body? I commenced treatment with a very stiff neck from the whiplash, and was very uncomfortable as I lay in various positions. During the first week I used my son's car and drove myself, until the windscreen blew out as I drove at 40 mph. I thought someone had shot me – I was beginning to think there was a plot by some higher being to get me up to heaven.

After treatment I used to go back to the shop, and we had a camp bed put out at the back. I would have a nap for one hour and after that I was fine and raring to go.

It was during this time that I practised visualisation. For me, I felt it put me in control of my body, and it was something I felt happy to do. However, it had to have a light-hearted feel to it. I used to imagine that above my head was a very large shiny brass gong and an army of little smurfs (well, I said it had to be light-hearted) all dressed like Roman soldiers complete with headgear and pikes. The light from the gong reflected on to my body like the warm sun, and as the gong was struck the soldiers would start marching up and down my body, squashing the little cancer cells, which looked remarkably like grey fried eggs with big frog-like eyes! When I gave my husband an account of my visualisation he suggested that perhaps I ought not to tell anyone in case they thought I had lost my marbles.

Although I was able to do this for myself, I still felt alone. Even though I had the support of a loving family and friends, I needed to talk about my fears and ask questions of someone who had experienced the same thing.

I was not to wait long. I had to knock at a neighbour's house. I hadn't seen Roz for months and months and she said that she had been ill with cancer. I told her that I too had just joined the club. She asked whether I would like to go along with her to 'Sue's House' at Ilford. This was a support group started by Terry Quirk, whose wife had died from cancer but had had so much support from the Bristol Cancer Help Centre that he decided to open his house on Wednesday evenings to cancer patients and their carers. When we arrived I could not believe my eyes. The house was at bursting point, with people all sitting around drinking pineapple and apple juice, presided over by Terry. I always felt that if he had a 12-foot scarf he would make a good double for Dr Who. He was aided by Katerina Collins, who herself had had breast cancer about nine years previously, and despite not having a good prognosis had survived with the help of Bristol and a holistic doctor.

My first impression was that it was not for me, and that all this love and peace was not going to help me fight my cancer. I was asked whether I would like healing, which I eagerly accepted, and at 9 o'clock we all held hands and said a prayer (non-denominational) for all those present and absent. It didn't matter what faith you were, if any: all were welcome. Halfway through the evening I was hooked. Katerina was a marvellous counsellor and Terry was such a happy person. You have French and Saunders of the Comic Club, but we had Collins and Quirk of the Cancer Club: a hard act for anyone to follow. I then introduced a friend, Maureen, from Ken's running club, who was in need of support after her operation, and we decided to go to Bristol together for a one-day session. We went down by train with our overnight bags, as accommodation had been arranged at a nearby hotel. We were both feeling very well – it was September and we had finished our treatments. To look at us you would never have believed where we were going.

We all met at the appointed time in the lounge at Grove House [part of BCHC premises], with its relaxing sun-lounger chairs – it was easy to relax and nod off to sleep. Unfortunately, not everyone looked as well as Maureen and I did. It was a wonderful day and we came away feeling good about ourselves, with our list of vitamins to take. As I was already on a gluten-free diet I didn't think I could carry out the Bristol diet completely, but promised myself I would cut out most of the red meats. If you start to feel guilty because you are eating something that is not on the Bristol food list, then that isn't going to do you any good. So I decided that I would be sensible about what I ate but that I would still have the odd tipple and the occasional steak – for I am a social animal, and the thought of giving up going out to restaurants and socialising wasn't something I relished. You have to do what is right for you.

When I was at Bristol I was asked whether I would be agreeable to being included in a five-year survey of breast cancer patients. I was only too pleased if it would help to improve breast cancer survival, and hoped that I would be around in five years to hear the results. Little did I know what I was letting myself in for. Every so often I was sent a form which I duly completed, although I felt it was not asking enough of the relevant questions – is there anyone else like me that finds it difficult to fill in those little boxes without wanting to say more? I always have a BUT!

Life started to return to normal. Vanessa was 16 years of age and about to start college, and Tony was 20 years old. He had no hesitation in thinking that I would get through all right. But Vanessa did not say much about it, and I found it difficult to press the subject with her. It is only now that I've felt able to discuss it with her, and she said she never realised at the time that women could die of breast cancer. I have had to advise her that she must be more 'breast aware' because of the family history. Ken has always been my rock – supportive about whatever I do. He came to Sue's House with me a few times, and as a carer was able to have the chance to say how he felt.

We soon had another worker at Sue's House – Frank – who came as a carer. He soon became our Treasurer and we found that he was good at raising money. Before long Terry's house was becoming too small to hold everyone; he had remarried and started a new family. A house was found and bought in the name of the North East London Cancer Help Centre (Sue's House). The house is now paid for, and in 1994 we celebrated ten years of Sue's House as a support group. Sadly Katerina died a few years ago, but was very much in our thoughts.

In September 1990 the results of the Bristol survey were announced. I was astounded. I could not believe what I heard. For a start, what about the five years it was supposed to take? I felt I had to do something. Similar thoughts were being voiced elsewhere, and contact was made with other women included in the survey. It's amazing how quickly things happen when you get like-minded people together. Before long the Bristol Survey Support Group was born – the rest is history. The culmination of our efforts was the film *Cancer Positive* that we made in the *Free for All* series on Channel 4, shown on 2 April 1992. I had the film crew following me for seven hours: at home, in Wanstead Park and – much to the amusement of the customers – in our shop! They were a terrific crew and we all felt it was worth while, especially when Heather Goodare and Isla Bourke questioned Professor McVie of the Cancer Research Campaign and Sir Walter Bodmer of the Imperial Cancer Research Fund.

At last we were getting somewhere, and the final step was the request to the Charity Commissioners for an investigation, and then the wait for their report.

You see, Bristol taught us to fight back when the odds were against us – and that's exactly what we did. Although the BSSG has been officially wound up, we still meet occasionally on a social basis. After all we went through we are not likely to cut ties.

Over the years my arthritis has given me more trouble than the cancer, and in December 1994 my rheumatologist suggested a chest Xray to see if my airways were affected. When I went back for the results, she stunned Ken and me with the news that a lesion was showing up on my sixth rib on the left side. Arrangements were made for a bone scan (I had one in May 1992, which was clear). The results showed up spots on both the left and right sixth ribs. I have now been prescribed the anti-oestrogen drug tamoxifen, and hopefully this will contain the disease. In my mind I was waiting to celebrate ten years free of cancer – that was my magic number, although you learn to live with the fact that it may return at any time. After getting over the initial shock, I realised that I had to pick myself up and remember all that Bristol and Sue's House had taught me.

At the present moment I feel very laid back (I'm not biting my nails down to the quick; neither have I lost weight with worry). Except for the usual problems of running a business during the recession, I enjoy a good family and social life and great holidays with friends, and I think that is all in my favour.

I have learnt to live with cancer and arthritis. I control my body. It doesn't control me. With that attitude it is easier for my family and friends to deal with it.

I find that running a needlecraft shop it is at times like a social services department. Obviously quite a few women know about my health problems through the film, the local paper and the 'grapevine'. They might ask for information on Bristol if they have a relative with cancer, but also a few cups of tea have been drunk in our back room to reassure worried women who have found a lump and/or have been diagnosed with cancer.

Nowadays with earlier diagnosis and better treatment for breast cancer, women can be more optimistic.

2 Peak Experiences

Geraldine Bloor

Geraldine lives and works in Wales. Diagnosed in 1986 at the age of 38, together with Rachel, Vicki, Joan, Joanna and Hilary, she represents the younger women who formed such a large proportion of the 'cases' in the Bristol study as compared with the 'controls'.

When I was asked to write my story, my first reaction was that it was neither special nor worthy of the privilege of becoming part of a book. When I told this to my sister Jayne she disagreed, and proceeded to remind me of all the possible benefits to others of my experience, and of all my achievements since having cancer. The following day I was walking the mountains with Jayne, her husband and a group of friends and business colleagues. It was a tough walk and Roger, one of the group, ten years my junior and 2 stone overweight, was having difficulty climbing the hills. He knew my history and told me how much he admired my determination and strength. Comparing myself to Roger on that day made me feel perhaps I did undervalue my life's achievements, and did not acknowledge the milestones I had reached and passed.

In 1984, at 36 years of age, I was introduced to rambling by a friend. I found myself at a loose end, and trying to rebuild my life after a failed marriage and a further failed relationship. At this time I was alone with two young children, eleven and nine years old, a full-time job, a house to run, and a large garden to tend.

I love the outdoors. I am writing this in March 1995, sitting in my garden in a sleeping bag. I am home from work with a virus, but cannot bear to be shut indoors when the sun shines; if it becomes cold I will retreat to my greenhouse.

In autumn 1985 I was feeling extremely tired and low in spirits. I felt out of control of my mind to the point where I asked a friend and colleague how I could obtain the services of a psychiatrist without becoming a statistic of my own office (I am an administrator in a social work office dealing with mental health). Thankfully, it never did come to this. In retrospect I can see that

18

the state of my physical and mental health at this time was due to my body utilising its resources to fight the cancer then growing undetected in my body.

It was in November 1985 that I went to my GP. I had been suffering from pain in my chest and arm over a period of weeks, and it seemed to be worsening. The final attack that sent me seeking help felt like a hot fluid trickling down the inside of my arm, leaving it feeling weak. I thought I was suffering from angina or something similar. My GP, however, found a pea-sized lump deep in my armpit, though my breast appeared normal. At this time cancer was not a consideration; my GP told me cancer never started with pain, and never started in the armpit! He referred me to a general surgeon, who wanted to operate to investigate the lump.

In the meantime, in early February 1986, I went on my annual skiing holiday. It was the first time I had taken the children. Matthew loved every minute; Becci hated it. Becci was nervous; I felt very tired, and was now feeling pain in my back and chest, so as a result she did not receive the support she needed; she lost all confidence and now cannot be enticed back to the slopes at any price. This is one of my greatest regrets. When I returned from skiing my hospital admission date awaited me – two days later.

In the December of 1985 my mother, who frequently suffered cysts in her breasts, had telephoned to say the latest lump was cancerous. As a result she was to undergo a mastectomy. However, it was found that the cancer was too far advanced for surgery, and she was sent home.

Eventually I had a lump removed from my breast, and lymph glands removed from my armpit. Five days after my operation I was taken to one side and told the lump was malignant and I would need to attend the specialist cancer clinic. I think the doctor was a little taken aback when all I could say was, 'How do I tell my mother, who herself has recently been diagnosed as suffering from breast cancer?' He went off to make me a cup of tea.

By the time he returned I had looked at the snow-covered hills and decided the first thing I would do was to put my name down for the following year's skiing trip. Cancer was not going to beat me. All I wanted to do was to leave hospital and go home. At this time I did not know much about my mother's cancer: Christmas had quickly followed, and then my skiing holiday and, since I was still feeling very tired, it had taken all my resources to organise these events. She and my sister visited me in hospital, 20 miles away. My mother was herself very tired and weak, and kept complaining that she must be putting on weight as she could not fasten her skirt. I learnt later she had actually visited me wearing two skirts. We all found this hilarious until several weeks later, when we learnt the cancer had attacked her bones and this could have led to confusion – the probable cause of the two skirts.

I cannot recall much about the following weeks. I remember my GP visiting me on my return from hospital and telling me I should explain my illness to my children. This was very difficult; I did not want to frighten them. I remember them shrugging their shoulders and walking away. I felt very hurt, but they did not know how to cope – what was cancer to them?

I remember opening the door one morning to find a potted plant sitting there, such a brightly coloured young plant. I don't know why, but that one plant meant the world to me. I remember the offers of help from neighbours, friends, colleagues; the never-ending thoughtfulness, care and concern of the ambulance crews who took me on the 70-mile daily round trip for treatment. I also remember the doctor who assumed I could impose on those I knew to undertake this chore, and the district nurse who told me I could not possibly have cancer, since 'they would have removed your breast'. (She happened to be the same nurse who eventually arranged the ambulance transport.)

I remember reading everything about cancer I could lay my hands on. I visited my hairdresser so frequently I should have taken up residence. Each time I would say 'take a little bit more off', until she told me there was nothing more to cut, and my sister went to work telling everyone I looked like a convict. I suppose this was one area I could control; perhaps I believed I was having the cancer cut away – I was certainly not conscious of this at the time, but have since often laughed about it at the hairdresser's.

During this period and the months that followed the foundations of a lasting friendship were laid with a work colleague. We had always had a friendly, flirtatious relationship, but suddenly he was offering the emotional support I so needed. This was to last for many, many months.

I was having to travel 70 miles a day, five days a week, for six weeks, to receive the radiotherapy treatment I was told I needed. Thankfully, I suffered no side effects other than tiredness, and the ambulance crews always did their best to help me through the endless waiting and travelling.

It was while I was attending the out-patient clinic that my mother, no longer able to cope with her pain, was admitted as an in-patient. She had asked for help which we could not provide. Hospital seemed the answer, but had I known then what I was soon to learn, and had the knowledge I was later to acquire of cancer in general, of the availability of services, of options open to cancer sufferers – I would never have taken her to hospital, even a specialist one.

I truly believe my mother knew she was dying. I didn't; my sister didn't. I think my father did but did not want to face it. My mother had been a nurse all her life and was very matter-of-fact. She resented intrusion and, though very ill, was furious when she learnt that my sister and I had spoken to her doctor. When she died some ten days later we found that she and my father had put all the paperwork in apple-pie order ready for THE day.

One consolation, if there can be any, was that in the days leading to my mother's death I was able to visit her every day. The ambulance crew always knew where to find me, as did the radiotherapy staff.

My mother was not the only member of the family to suffer from cancer. Her sister (several years her junior) had undergone two mastectomies, the first some 20 years earlier than these events. She is still alive today and in relatively good health.

In September 1987 their mother, my maternal grandmother, was six weeks away from celebrating her hundredth birthday when she too died. The death certificate read 'carcinoma': not 'natural causes' or 'old age'. She had always been a lively lady who kept good health, but latterly had become very frail and had lived in a home for about 12 to 18 months. We had been told in the summer that she had developed breast cancer.

Because of my family history I was kept under very close scrutiny, attending the cancer clinic at frequent intervals, but this did not help with the next phase of my life.

From July 1986 I had complained of discomfort in my lower abdomen. I had been examined and nothing was found. In April 1987 a female cancer specialist decided I ought to have a pelvic scan. I waited for the results but nothing came. My GP, after a routine visit, decided he would follow it up for me. Later that day I had a telephone call to say the specialist wanted to see me urgently, as he thought I had cancer again. It was in the middle of August that I had my next operation – a total hysterectomy. Apparently the same tumour that had been present in my breast had travelled by a not so well-known route from my breast to my ovaries.

Between these operations I had tried to resume walking, but I was weak and still tired. I did, however, manage my annual skiing trip with a friend and my son. After my second operation my medication was changed. I suffered from weight gain, swollen knees, sleepless nights. When I tried to resume walking I found I had no stamina and could not even cross a stile without great difficulty because of my knees. I blamed the medication, which was changed several times, but it took years of persistence before the dosage was dropped to an acceptable level.

Again, in retrospect, I can see that perhaps some of the symptoms and side effects I suffered were more a result of the total hysterectomy and subsequent hormone changes than the medication, but no one ever discussed this with me. During the first twelve months after this operation I could count on one hand the number of good nights' sleep I had. My normal night was to visit the toilet two or three times and be unable to sleep because my knee joints ached like toothache. It was not unknown for me to sleep on the floor with my legs draped up and over the edge of the bed; for some reason this sometimes alleviated the discomfort.

During the 18 months between these operations my personal life had seen some highs and some lows. The special friendship with the colleague mentioned earlier had developed, and begun to dwindle. He was a little younger than me, and married with two very young children. During this period he left his wife, went to live with his mother, returned home, left again to come and live with me, and eventually returned home again because he missed his children. I have been told by a mutual friend that it was obvious how deeply he felt for me. Through all the upheaval we remained not only colleagues at work but also very good friends, and I hope are still so to this day, though we are now more distant.

I mention this because it was another milestone, another of life's unplanned challenges that have to be overcome. People have always said they do not know how I coped through my illness – I had always accepted it in such a matter-of-fact way. Initially, I attributed it to being more concerned about my mother; then there was my attitude that cancer was not going to kill me, especially after taking my mother. I also think the support and love of this relationship helped; it was not without its hardships and its problems but I still felt needed, accepted and loved by someone despite the physical scarring. This really was insignificant compared with what it might have been, but it was still significant to me.

I had come through, and although initially cancer was always in the back of my mind, I believed I had beaten it. The only time I was overtaken by fear was when the provider of my love and emotional support was taken ill himself with suspected hepatitis. My only means of contact was via a friend, but when someone telephoned his wife to ask about him, she mistakenly believed it was me. She issued an ultimatum which signalled the end of the relationship as it had been, and I sank to an all-time low. It was about four months before I could face the world again, having had to stand alone for the first time since having cancer diagnosed.

After my first operation in 1986 I read a lot about cancer and I became particularly interested in the connections made by some to lifestyle. I realised that since the break-up of my marriage ten years earlier, although I had survived and survived well, I had carried a lot of responsibility and been under a lot of pressure much of the time – like the occasion when a representative of the then Department of Health and Social Security knocked on my door at about 6 o'clock one evening and informed me that I owed them over £100. After talking to him at length it transpired that *they* owed *me* over £100. I soon learnt to stand on my own feet and fight for my rights.

At work I had friends who were interested in alternative therapies, and it was one of these who suggested the Bristol Cancer Help Centre to me. My sister told me later that my mother had been considering attending the Centre but death had come too quickly. She gave me the book *Getting Well Again* by Carl and Stephanie Simonton, and I sent for information on the work of the Cancer Help Centre. I also attended meetings of a local group based on the same lines as Bristol. It was in July 1986 that I went to Bristol. I was in good general health, but weak and tired. I had never actually been *ill*; I had felt overtired and lacking in energy and vitality, but had never considered myself sick. Although it was a financial struggle, with the help of a bursary I went to Bristol for one week with a friend.

The peace and tranquillity experienced on entering the building was immeasurable. For one week I was free of the pressures of the outside world. I could concentrate on myself, absorb the calm and love, and think about my life. I owe much to the Cancer Help Centre, and although I no longer religiously follow any of their therapies, they continue to influence my life and my thoughts.

I practise what I feel is appropriate when I feel I need it. I try not to let the outside world take over my life completely; I try to step off the merry-go-round before it goes too fast for me.

Of the patients who were in Bristol with me (together with their supporters) at least three are now dead (one of them a breast cancer sufferer); a fourth had travelled from Canada for her visit to the Cancer Centre and I lost contact with her after a while; and I did not maintain contact at all with a fifth. Of those I kept in touch with, even those that have since died, I would not hesitate to say that they all benefited enormously from their visit to the Centre and would have recommended it to anyone. Some people will die anyway, but if Bristol only gave them tranquillity in their last weeks or months then it was of benefit, and not only to the cancer sufferer but to the carers, relatives and friends also.

I know I appreciated my time in Bristol and am thankful for what I learnt, and am certain I could say the same for those who were there with me. Had I had the resources I would have liked very much to have continued practising the therapies I had been introduced to, and I would have liked to attend the Centre on a regular basis; unfortunately, I could not afford this. I continued to attend the local group running along the same lines as Bristol for some time.

Today, it is now early July 1995 (it has taken me a long time to piece my story together). Once again I am sitting in my garden enjoying a pleasant summer's evening, listening to the water falling from the fountain in my pond. The pond is in its second year and is looking well established (a friend's husband dug it out because he wanted the soil, and I did the rest). I am pleased with it; my garden is my haven, my tranquillity.

It is now nine years since I was diagnosed as suffering from breast cancer and, although I feel I suffer far more health problems now than I ever did before being diagnosed, I am generally very fit and active. I have just returned from a weekend in Killarney, walking with the same group mentioned earlier. We climbed the second highest peak in Ireland, some 3,000 feet. However, this time Roger was ahead of me and carrying my rucksack – oh dear, I had better lose some weight and go back to the gym to get fit. We hope to spend a weekend walking in Snowdonia shortly. I do find life tougher than I used to, but I am getting older, as people keep reminding me. My children are now 22 and 20 years old: Becci has just been awarded a diploma in Business and Finance, Matthew has just completed his first year of a business course at Cardiff. I still have my full-time job, my large garden and my house to maintain; life is still a struggle.

I realise that the stage at which a cancer is diagnosed is important, as is the general state of health of the patient. However, I am a great believer in attitude and usually feel that anything is possible if you want it enough and believe in it. Perhaps I was just lucky and my cancer was diagnosed early, but looking at the time lapses in my record between initial contact and diagnosis, and then diagnosis and treatment, it could so easily have been different.

I was in good health before being diagnosed with cancer, I had never been an 'ill' person, and I was fairly active. Now, nine years on, although carrying more weight than I would like, I still consider myself to be fit and active and ready to face most challenges.

3 Immune Response

Rachel Charles

Rachel is a British Association for Counselling (BAC) Accredited Counsellor and Psychosynthesis therapist working in p⸍ivate practice. She lives in a quiet village in Suffo⸍k with her husband, Springer spaniel and cat. Aged 43 at diagnosis in 1986, she took part in the film *Cancer Positive* (1992) and is the author of several books. Her most absorbing hobbies are organic gardening and playing the cello.

'Tea or coffee, madam? Excuse me, madam ....', but I hadn't heard. My forehead was pressed hard against the small, thick window of the plane, as I strained to see the misty, snow-capped peaks below. The captain had just been describing the route: '... and on the left you will see the highest mountain in the Alps: Mont Blanc'. My heart lurched. Somewhere trapped beneath the ice lay the body of my brother. He had vanished without trace while approaching the summit some years previously, along with his two climbing companions. I recalled our last meeting when he had turned up unexpectedly in London after driving over from Gloucester, where he was practising as a doctor. He had talked enthusiastically about his future plans for research into heart disease. Imprinted for ever on my memory is his final farewell: his wave, his infectious grin, his relaxed, athletic figure opening the door to his green Beetle. During the days when we had shared a flat together he had become my closest friend, the only person to whom I could entrust my deepest feelings and thoughts. To lose my dear brother was truly terrible, like losing part of myself. Since the accident my dreams had been tortured by desperate searches through cold, slippery terrain, faced by impossible rock faces or peering down terrifying precipices. But he was nowhere to be found, and I awoke with the sobs seeping into my pillow.

'Madam ...' The stewardess's brightly painted face came into view. I shook my head dumbly, choking back the tears and, as always, making a big effort to look normal. I would have to get a grip on myself. This was no time to be overcome by emotions. My flight to Italy was purely for business purposes. As managing editor for a publisher, it was my job to see our latest books on to the presses, and it was going to be high-pressure, nerve-racking work, straight to the printer on arrival and up at 5am tomorrow for last-minute checking of ozalid proofs. Idle machines cost a small fortune and I knew from experience that the printers would be standing over me, ready to snatch the pages from my hands as soon as they were passed. It was best not to think about the amount of money involved if I made a mistake.

There was a notebook in my handbag, which I took out and opened. In it I was recording my stress levels, becoming increasingly concerned by the growing catalogue of events that were in some way fearful. There was good reason for this project. Just a few months previously, my health had cracked under the strain and I was shocked to find myself with breast cancer, or rather 'primary carcinoma' as my surgeon had called it. He himself was very caring, and assured me that the rest of the treatment would consist of radiotherapy to the breast area and nearby lymph nodes only, to mop up any escaped malignant cells. The consultant oncologist, however, had a different approach; she began to put considerable pressure on me to have my ovaries irradiated. I can recall her now, all bright and chatty, perched elegantly on the couch, wearing a vivid floral sundress. She laid her hand on my arm and told me that because of my relative youth, the chances of recurrence of the cancer were slightly higher. By bringing on the menopause artificially and lowering the oestrogen levels, my prognosis would be improved. Moreover, I must decide quickly – within a week. She fluttered out of the consulting room. I was appalled. I hadn't been married long and was still clutching on to the hope of a last-minute baby. Suddenly all chances of motherhood were being snatched from me. The tears rose in my throat. How could I make such an important decision in so short a time? What if I refused the treatment – would I be risking my life? What statistics were there to guide me? I desperately sought further information from the hospital, but none was forthcoming.

In the end I appealed for more time in which to make this important decision, but was firmly told that I could only receive the treatment within the next five weeks. I am not a naturally suspicious person, but this seemed very strange. Why could I not return in, say, three months for the radiation menopause? It was only after persistent questioning that a junior doctor finally admitted the truth: a trial was being conducted to see if there was any difference in survival rates between those women who had their ovaries irradiated and those who had chemotherapy, or those who had neither. Clearly, my number had been picked to have my ovaries zapped, which, as I later discovered, was not standard procedure – especially as no test had been carried out on my breast tissue to see whether the cancer was in fact hormone-related. So the intention had been to use me as a guinea pig, totally without my knowledge. I was furious. This consultant had deceived me and as a result had put me under immense stress. It was bad enough dealing with the emotional impact of a life-threatening illness, but such a betrayal was devastating. It was with huge relief that I heard about the Cancer Help Centre in Bristol. After speaking to the resident doctor on the telephone, I knew that here were the people I could trust; this was the route to follow. Thus I found the courage to refuse the additional hospital treatment.

However, there was another major worry. After the lumpectomy and radiotherapy I had had a routine bone scan, the results of which were unclear. A 'hot spot' had shown up across my left ribs, which, I was told, was either something insignificant, or else indicated that the cancer had already invaded my skeleton. This news had thrown me into total panic. Suddenly, at the age of 43, I was face to face with my own mortality, but I wasn't ready to die. My intuition told me that dramatic changes to my way of life were essential if I was to make a good recovery and remain well, but this wasn't easy. I had a husband out of work and, in addition to all the normal bills, a mortgage to pay on a house that was subsiding and in urgent need of expensive repairs.

During my week's stay at the Cancer Help Centre, a notion had been introduced which had made a deep impression on me: you don't have to become the helpless victim of this terrifying disease; rather, you can experience cancer as a turning point in life, providing the opportunity for creative change. Although I had done relatively well in my publishing career, I found it strangely unfulfilling. Most of the time I was too exhausted to enjoy its good moments – long hours were the norm and I was well aware that if I wasn't prepared to put in unpaid overtime most days, there was no hope of promotion. Moreover, the business ethics depressed me; the overriding goal was to make a profit, so that quality inevitably suffered and worthwhile ideas were often thrown out.

My counsellor at Bristol had been an inspiration, encouraging me to look at the areas of my life that needed mending. He himself had suffered a tumour near his spine, which had affected his movement to the point where he wondered if he would ever walk again. In addition, the radiotherapy had burnt out part of his lung. Not to be defeated, he had taken up singing, which had restored much of its capacity. To look at him now, it was hard to imagine how ill he had been and I greatly admired the strength of his spirit. It had been his suggestion to monitor my stress levels. He had also encouraged me to express anger safely. Classically, cancer patients find themselves in a trapped situation, often feeling hopeless and helpless, yet unable to say how they feel or to ask for what they want. Over time, resentment builds up and strong emotions such as anger and grief become turned inwards, frequently resulting in depression and despair. Often patients have suffered a bereavement of a close family member or friend, from which they have been unable to recover. My present tears reminded me that the pain of my brother's death was still raw.

This portrait of the typical cancer patient bore an uncanny resemblance to myself – but could emotional states really have anything to do with malignant tumours? Being a natural bookworm, I decided to do some further investigations and set aside some time to visit the Central Medical Library in London. Here, among some research papers, I encountered a long, tongue-twisting word: psychoneuroimmunology, the science that explores the link between the mind and the immune system.[1] I was excited! Until recently it had been supposed that immunity was a completely separate system which responded directly to harmful organisms or errant cells, but there was now evidence that the chemicals known as neurotransmitters, which pass messages from one nerve cell to the next, could also regulate immunity. This was how it worked: lymphocytes (the white cells of the immune system) have been found to carry minute receptors that respond to a variety of neurotransmitters. It is therefore reasonable to deduce that messages received by these receptors from the brain can influence the ways in which the lymphocytes behave. Moreover, peripheral nerves have been identified that run out to the key organs of the immune system, the thymus gland, the spleen, the lymph nodes and the bone marrow. This was extremely significant. In plain words this meant that how you think and feel can have an effect on your immunity, and therefore on your susceptibility to disease.

I had reason to be so thrilled at this discovery. Since the opening of the Cancer Help Centre, there had been plenty of sceptics among the medical profession who had poured scorn on its complementary therapies. Yet experienced counsellors there had often been aware of the strong link between emotional and physical states among their patients. Here at last was solid evidence. Moreover, it was now quite plausible to suppose that the immune system could be influenced by positive thinking, that it could be encouraged to fend off invading pathogens more effectively and, yes, even to fight malignant cells with greater efficiency. I could indeed boost my own immunity!

While at the Centre, I had borrowed a book called *Getting Well Again* by Carl Simonton, a radiotherapist, and his wife Stephanie, a psychotherapist.[2] They had discovered that cancer patients fared significantly better if their treatment was supported by mental visualisation of their immune systems fighting the cancerous tumours. Patients conjured up their own protagonists, using whatever images worked best for them. It seemed that the processes of healing responded best to symbolic images straight from the unconscious, rather than to logical thought.

We were encouraged to practise this technique at Bristol, always preceded by deep physical relaxation after which we felt calm and receptive. To help clear my bones from any secondary spread, I imagined that my skeleton was a tall tree and that my white cells were a flock of doves. They investigated every branch for little black grubs (malignant cells) and pecked up those that they found. Their droppings fell to the earth and fertilised the tree, which grew big and strong. Daily practice was helping me to feel that I was the one in charge of my health.

Further reading led me to a study that corroborated the Simontons' work. Dr Barry L. Gruber of the Medical Illness Counseling Center in Chevy Chase, Maryland, USA, collaborated with Dr Nicholas R. Hall from the University of Florida to evaluate the benefits of relaxation combined with imagery.[3] For one year they tested the immune systems of adults with cancer who were regularly using these mental techniques. They were asked to create their own images of their white cells conquering the tumours. Throughout the year the doctors found that the action of the patients' lymphocytes became enhanced, that antibody production increased, that the natural killer cells could more effectively discharge their cell poisons and that there was improvement in the manufacture of interleukin 2 (which regulates the growth of immune cells). Interestingly, if the quality and quantity of relaxation and imagery were heightened, so were the immune changes, and if they were lessened, the alterations in immunity followed suit. This left me in no doubt that visualisation could be remarkably beneficial.

'Ladies and gentlemen, kindly fasten your seat belts. We are about to enter some turbulence,' announced the captain. As the plane lurched and rolled I realised that I must find a way to let my brother rest in peace, so that my own life could go forward. Rock climbing had been his passion and once he had even expressed the wish that his death place could be a mountain. What more magnificent monument to him than Mont Blanc! I held in my mind the fleeting glimpse I had had of his snowy resting place and sent him a prayer. I felt again our strong bond, was grateful for it, and as we flew further away, I gradually let him go.

While the therapies at the Cancer Help Centre had in no way promised any magic cure, the more research I did, the more evidence I accumulated that the programme was in fact offering natural methods of enhancing immunity, thus giving the body the best possible chances of fighting its own disease. This understanding gave me renewed hope and I vowed to maximise my opportunities for survival. Moreover, despite having achieved middle age, I still felt there was so much more to discover about myself. I had been going along on autopilot for too long and there was something missing. What could that be? It had to do with a need to find real meaning to my life – a point to my existence. It was unthinkable to die before unearthing what this was.

Having seen my firm's books on to the presses, it was now possible to take some time off work and make more visits to the library. The pieces were beginning to fit together. Further searches among psychological journals led me to a study presented to the Psychosomatic Society in Dallas in 1979 involving men whose wives had died of breast cancer.[4] The immune systems of these men were tested within the first month of their bereavement and it was found that the responsiveness of their lymphocytes had declined significantly. Even a year later, their immunity was still depressed in many cases. How wise of my counsellor to tell me gently that I must complete the mourning for my brother.

The more I discovered, the more fascinated I became by the immune system, and ideas for a book of my own began to form.

Perhaps if I combined everything I was discovering about this complex subject together with my personal experience of cancer, then it might give others hope too. Yes, this would be truly worthwhile. It seemed increasingly astonishing to me that practitioners of conventional medicine were so reluctant to talk to psychotherapists and those involved in complementary healthcare, when so much valuable understanding and information could be shared for the benefit of patients. It seemed equally obvious to me that, as people, we are whole beings, consisting not just of bodies but of feelings, mind and spirit also, so that if there is a lack in one area, then that will affect the workings of the entire organism. Getting better was not just about cutting out a malignant growth and killing off other errant cells with radiotherapy or chemotherapy; it was about healing our innermost being also.

My stress levels had shot up during the Italian trip, and to go on like this could, quite literally, prove fatal. At the Centre I had been taught that the body can most readily heal itself when in a state of complete relaxation, especially during meditation when the brain ticks over from the normal beta rhythms into the slower alpha rhythms. We had used biofeedback machines to test how well we were doing and I had been surprised at the ease with which I could switch into a deeply relaxed mode. Regular meditation, however, was still insufficient to offset the strains of my everyday existence and I had some serious decision-making in front of me. My stress notebook had filled rapidly and patterns were emerging. Work days were fraught with alarm. Here is an example:

Wednesday: 8.05 tube train too full to squeeze on to. Agitated about being late while waiting for the next. Felt terribly claustrophobic with people pushing and shoving. Had a confrontation with N. [our publishing director] this morning because B. [an uncooperative editor] had gone over budget, despite my diplomatic attempts to make checks. Angry to have to carry the can for her. Grabbed a sandwich at lunchtime and worked through. Traffic fumes in the city really terrible; could hardly breathe. Telephone kept ringing, making concentration very difficult. Worried because several books are behind schedule. One MS is so bad it will need complete rewriting. How can I keep both authors and bosses happy? Am sick of playing piggy in the middle.

At this afternoon's meeting N. actually proudly presented one of my best ideas as his own! Flabbergasted. If only we had a PD we could respect. R. [our managing director] hired him against everyone's advice, so now has to side with him. We get no support or encouragement. She hasn't even noticed that one-third of the creative team has left this company since she took over. Will I be next? I so hate office politics. Why can't we all work amicably together instead of each person trying to outdo the other?

Worked late till 7pm trying to catch up. Train stopped for ages in the tunnel without explanation. Could hear others rumbling by. Scared they would crash into us. Felt increasingly panic stricken.

Then a weird-looking man followed me up the High Street from the station. Frightened he would see where I lived, so took refuge in the late-night shop until he wandered off.

This made depressing reading. Moreover, I now knew from my researches what was happening to my body while suffering from repeated stress. Each situation which I perceived to be in some way alarming or fearful triggered physiological responses which prepared me to deal with the emergency by running away or fighting. My heart beat faster to pump the blood to the brain and large muscle groups. Perspiration was a sign that my cooling system had been set in motion, and my liver released extra sugar into my bloodstream to provide that necessary spurt of energy. Along with all this, hormones – namely adrenaline and the corticosteroids – were coursing around in my bloodstream acting as the chemical 'messengers'. Such reactions could have been life-saving in primitive times, faced with, say, a lion in the African bush. But our modern city jungles rarely provide the opportunity for physical expression of rage or terror. It was hardly appropriate to punch my boss on the nose (satisfying though that might have been on more than one occasion!), nor was there much I could do when trapped in a motionless tube train, except grin and bear it. Thus the hormones would circulate in the bloodstream to no purpose, and some of these, especially cortisol, are known to be powerful immunosuppressants. Hence the importance of keeping stress levels low if immunity is to remain high.

Hitherto I had taken it for granted that life was an ongoing struggle, but a new realisation was beginning to enter my consciousness – it needn't be like this! With the help of my

counsellor I began to form a vision of a new me. Part of my early
childhood had been spent in the depths of the countryside and
I had idyllic memories of climbing trees, rolling in haystacks
and lying in long grass gazing up at the sky. Now I had an intense
yearning for country life, for its peacefulness, its fresh air and
natural beauty. But there was a difficult sticking point: my
husband adamantly refused to move out of London.

I tried to explain how important this was to me; that my body
felt poisoned by the foul air; that, to stay well, it was essential to
reduce my stress levels; that to continue with my city existence
seemed like a death sentence to me. Here was a fundamental
difference between us: he argued that he would vegetate in the
country, would be unable to pursue his particular hobbies and
interests, and would therefore be miserable. In the end we settled
on a compromise. We would sell the house in East Finchley and
find somewhere on the edge of London which at least had access
to some countryside. Over the next few months we sifted through
hundreds of estate agents' particulars and eventually decided on
a well-built ex-council house bordering on Epping Forest.
Meanwhile we had essential repairs carried out at home and
spent any spare moments touching up decorations. The sale
raised twice the cost of the other house, so the difference could
be invested. With the security of a small private income I was at
last able to take the risk of working freelance.

My husband had found my illnesss extremely difficult to cope
with. Hitherto I had been the strong one, taking on the major
responsibilities. Now my life was threatened and there was a
sudden reversal, asking, perhaps, too much of him and therefore
putting considerable strain on our relationship. Cancer can be a
grossly unwelcome intruder into the entire family system. For this
reason, the Bristol Centre wisely offers special support to partners
and close family members of patients, encouraging them to
become involved in the programme also.

After the move, each day started with a jog accompanied by my
labrador, Zuki. I had learnt that bouncing movements help to keep
the lymph circulating – important because, unlike the bloodstream,
this system has no pump of its own. Thus those vital white
immunity cells were being speedily delivered wherever they were
most needed. There was a route up the back roads to the forest
edge, leading into a network of paths. How the atmosphere
changed as soon as I entered the first line of trees! Gone was the
bedlam of street life and the honking chaos of traffic. Instead I

could tune in to the sweet trills of birdsong, the scurrying of small wild animals and the gentle rustling of leaves. Here I felt protected by the stout trunks and overhanging branches. Here I could open my lungs and breathe deeply without the fear of further poisoning from atmospheric pollution. This became my healing place.

Once more my instincts were proving right and the more research I did the more I respected the needs of my body. In addition to causing some cancers directly from tiny particulates, many exhaust fumes still contain lead, a poisonous heavy metal which, when breathed in, enters the system and depresses immunity.[5] Trees, however, have a cleansing effect by giving off oxygen during the process of photosynthesis. Equally, malignant cells have a hard time surviving in well-oxygenated tissue; they much prefer an anaerobic environment (one that is without oxygen).

A particular feature of the programme at Bristol had been the diet. This had come under fire from some quarters of the medical establishment as being too stringent, and indeed patients with cancers of the bowel or stomach generally found the amount of roughage too much to cope with. Such cases were always treated individually, and tender chicken or fish replaced the beans and lentils of the vegan fare. Those of us with high protein requirements or poor digestion were made delicious soya shakes, with tofu and bananas or other fruits. I have been a lifelong sufferer from hypoglycaemia (low blood sugar), and therefore extra protein around mid-morning is essential to prevent a crash in my blood sugar, with accompanying dizziness, blurred vision and other unpleasant symptoms. The soya shakes sorted that out instantly. Indeed, the personal attention and care that each of us experienced at Bristol made us feel loved and special.

The Bristol diet had been based on the ideas of Dr Max Gerson, who not only cured Albert Schweitzer of his diabetes, but became famous for his successful treatment of cancer patients, achieving improved prognoses and even cure in some cases. Referring to the adulterated, refined diet of the time, he maintained that a body fed on such unnatural stuff 'loses the harmony and cooperation of the cells, finally its natural defences, immunity and healing power'.[6] Instead, he emphasised organically grown raw vegetables and fruit, rich in nutrients. Clearly, it was time I gave up the quick-to-prepare convenience food and learnt to nourish myself properly. So out went the packets and tins, the high-fat dairy products, the red meat, all refined breads, cakes and sugar, jams, added salt and the coffee and tea, along with my ancient, pock-marked aluminium pans (another metal that depresses immunity); and in came the fresh salads, vegetables and fruit, whole grains, lentils, beans, tofu, nuts and seeds, herb teas and stainless steel for cooking. I rarely ate meat anyway, so this was easy to give up, as were sticky cakes which I found too sickly, but the hardest of all was cheese. I loved that wonderful salty, tangy taste and used to eat it every day – lots of it – often trying out different varieties. Besides, it was so versatile and convenient: cheese sandwiches, cheese on toast, cauliflower cheese, not to mention that little piece of Brie or Camembert to round off a good dinner. Yes, that really was a considerable sacrifice. But there were compensations in the form of newly introduced ingredients and I had fun experimenting with recipes such as millet patties, almond and lentil burgers, bean and grain casserole, nut roast, and cakes free of refined sugar such as molasses cookies and date squares. There was one major drawback, however, and that was the time needed to prepare the vegan food, which often demanded much washing, chopping, grating and grinding. Even salads were more complicated: seeds and beans were specially sprouted, being rich in vitamins, and 'five-star' raw vegetables like broccoli, grated carrot and beetroot with homemade dressing were preferred to the usual pieces of limp lettuce, couple of tomatoes and dollop of Heinz salad cream. Happily, I found some herb teas that I genuinely liked and was soon so addicted to peppermint tea that I was unable to start the day without it. Top priority was to get myself well, however much effort this required. Somehow I was going to have to find the courage to go back for that repeat scan. Taking my healing in hand helped me to feel in control.

Moreover, I was now delving into the benefits of vitamins and minerals, and was beginning to appreciate the excellence of the nutritional content of the Bristol diet. There was a special emphasis on orange-yellow vegetables and fruits, such as carrots, apricots, pumpkins and melon, as well as dark-green vegetables. These contain beta-carotene (vitamin A), essential for the production of the white B- and T-cells that are the main fighting troops of the immune system. Indeed, the carrot juice before meals had become something of a joke and Bristol patients were reputed to turn yellow. This was an exaggeration; the doctor suggested that we watch the colour of our palms for a tanned look, and to cut back on the vitamin A when this point was reached. It is interesting that recent research has shown that beta-carotene protects against breast cancer in younger women.[7] Here again, scientific research is only just catching up on knowledge acquired from experience by complementary practitioners.

Of the B vitamins, I discovered that pyridoxine (B_6) was the most important for successful immune functioning, working in cooperation with vitamin B_2 for the formation of antibodies. It was found in many of the foods recommended in the diet: wheat germ, brown rice, molasses, avocado pears, soya beans, sunflower seeds, walnuts, spinach and other dark-green vegetables. Additionally, all of this group are helpful to people under stress and the complex was given to patients as a supplement along with vitamins A and C.

Nobel-prizewinner Dr Linus Pauling has been a controversial figure, having been the recipient of as much scorn as praise. While some call him a crank, others regard him as a genius. Nevertheless, his treatment of cancer patients with vitamin C in excess of 10 grams (a little over $1/3$ oz) daily showed a marked improvement in prognosis.[8] It has since been demonstrated that this vitamin stimulates the activity of macrophages, the large white blood cells that gobble up invaders and help to fight tumours. An even more recent study suggests that it encourages antibodies to respond to tumours and that it aids in the production of T killer cells, which attack the malignant cells directly with a poison.[9]

The trace element selenium is known to be very protective against cancer and for this reason it was also prescribed as a supplement. British soil tends to be low in this mineral, so that our wheat is less rich in it than, say, American. It promotes immune functioning in a number of ways, especially by protecting the large white macrophages and reinforcing their ability to reduce tumours. Like zinc, it assists in the excretion of immunosuppressing heavy metals from the body, such as cadmium, lead and mercury. Brazil nuts, which we generally found in our morning muesli at Bristol, are one of the most reliable sources of selenium.

Zinc is vital for effective immunity and significantly assists in the production of those white T-cells. Since chemical fertilisers bind it up in the soil, we are becoming more deficient in this mineral as modern farming practices develop. It is further removed in food refining and the boiling of vegetables. How wise therefore, to eat those greens organically grown, fresh and raw – or, at the most, just lightly steamed.

The more I read about nutrition, the more I realised how important the diet was for the promotion of really good health, so the extra work involved became less of a chore, and I chopped, ground and grated enthusiastically. Within a fortnight I had lost 7lb in weight, which delighted me, and I have stayed at a modest 9 stone ever since. Then there have been other unexpected bonuses: my skin is beautifully clear, my joints feel permanently well oiled and even my brain ticks over with greater clarity.

Although my researches had proved to me that the Bristol regime, far from being airy-fairy nonsense, was in fact positively helping me to fight any malignancy by boosting my immune system, I nevertheless felt increasingly nervous as the appointment for the repeat bone scan drew closer. I had already witnessed the ravages of cancer among companion sufferers: the bones gradually disintegrating, often causing agonising pain, with death sometimes a blessed relief when the cancer finally attacks one of the vital organs. I am not a particularly brave person and have a poor tolerance of pain; I didn't want to die like this. In the end I gave myself another month of total dedication to the Bristol system. I meditated three times daily, visualised the healing of the 'hot spot', took up aerobics, poured out my feelings to my counsellor, played my cello as often as possible, stuck religiously to the vegan diet and spent a small fortune on vitamin pills.

When the day finally arrived I felt sick with apprehension and was grateful to my husband for agreeing to accompany me to the hospital. The routine involved injection with radioactive material which would take several hours to circulate through my system, after which the scan would be carried out. As I rolled up my sleeve, the nurse assured me that the injection was completely harmless and would eventually work its way out of my body. Doubtless she was doing her best to soothe me, but since it came from a canister with hazard warning signs all over it, this was somewhat difficult to believe. She asked me if I had any aches or pains and, without revealing my reasons, I was happy to say I had never felt better!

The intervening hours were spent in a nearby art gallery, where some enchanting Impressionist paintings provided a welcome distraction, transporting me, at least in imagination, to the landscape of rural France with its long lines of poplars and fields of ripe wheat. Back at the hospital I was placed in a room by myself and stood in front of a giant machine, which scanned me in three sections.

Then came the interminable waiting. After ten days the letter from my surgeon finally dropped on to our doormat. Taking a deep breath before opening it, and trying desperately to steady my shaking hands, I slowly took in the news. The letter was formal but friendly, explaining that the hot spot had now receded and there was definitely no evidence of secondary spread of the cancer to my bones. The relief was overwhelming. I felt as if I had just been given the best present ever – my life! How precious it was to me now. Never again would I take my health for granted; never again would I push myself so close to the edge of the grave. Henceforward I would treat my body with the care and attention it deserved. Thank you to all those dear, dedicated people at Bristol who pointed me in the right direction.

It is now almost ten years later and I remain well. Moreover, I have kept my promise to myself and still maintain the Bristol regime, although somewhat less rigorously. Stress levels have sometimes soared too high and those occasions have demanded real self-confrontation. Once more I came face to face with the question of medical ethics as I was one of the women in the bungled Bristol study. Yet again my confidence in the medical establishment was severely put to the test, and it was only by becoming involved in the campaign for our rights as patients that I was able to work through my feelings of outrage. Does the medical profession not appreciate how important it is for cancer patients not to be put under unnecessary strain?

Yet, without question, cancer was a true turning point for me and through it I was able to appreciate my life and find meaning to it. In the end I abandoned my career as an editor and turned to writing in the complementary health field. The publication of my two books *Mind, Body and Immunity* and *Food for Healing*[10] has enabled me to share with others my own knowledge and experience, which has proved deeply fulfilling. Meanwhile I retrained as a psychosynthesis[11] therapist and counsellor, and the work I now do with people is both challenging and rewarding.

Sadly, my first marriage was unable to withstand the emergence of this new me, and we eventually negotiated an amicable parting. I moved to the depths of the Suffolk countryside, a rolling, open landscape with the most magnificent skies, where the quality of life is high indeed. The most unexpected happening was the chance meeting of my present husband while demonstrating against the building of a further nuclear power station on our beautiful heritage coast. We jointly held up a protesting placard and shared our reasons for detesting all things that threaten our natural environment. We now live very happily together with our cat and dog amid a very lovely, totally organic garden.

Well, it's time to go out and water my vegetable plot. The runner beans are coming along fine.

Notes and References

1 Ader, R. (ed.) *Psychoneuroimmunology* 1981; San Diego, Calif.: Academic Press. See also Mestel, R. 'Let mind talk'. *New Scientist* 23 July 1994: 26–31.
2 Simonton, O.C., Matthews-Simonton, S. and Creighton, J.L. *Getting Well Again* 1980; New York: Bantam.
3 Gruber, B.L., Hall, N.R., Hersh, S.P. and Dubois, P. 'Immune system and psychological changes in metastatic cancer patients while using relaxation and guided imagery: a pilot study'. *Scandinavian Journal of Behavior Therapy* 1988; 17: 25–46.
4 Schleifer, S.J., Keller, S.E., Camerino, M., Thornton, J.C. and Stein, M. 'Suppression of lymphocyte stimulation following bereavement'. *Journal of the American Medical Association* 1983; 250: 374–77.
5 Parker, P. (ed.). 'Car pollution – the facts'. *Greenpeace News* Spring 1989.
6 Gerson, M. *A Cancer Therapy: results of fifty cases* 5th edn. 1990; Bonita, Calif.: Gerson Institute (first published 1958).
7 Lee, H.P., Gourley, L., Duffy, S.W., Estève, J.S., Lee, J. and Day, N.E. 'Dietary effects on breast-cancer risks in Singapore'. *Lancet* 1991; 337: 1197–1200.
8 Cameron, E. and Pauling, L. *Cancer and Vitamin C* 1980; London: Weidenfeld.
9 Holford, Patrick, 'Are you immune?' *Optimum Nutrition* Winter 1993: 28–35. See also Dunne, L.J. (ed.), Nutrition Search, Inc. *Nutrition Almanac* 3rd edn. 1990; New York: McGraw Hill.
10 Charles, Rachel *Mind, Body and Immunity* 2nd rev. edn 1996; London: Cedar/Heinemann (first published 1990). *Food For Healing* 1995; London: Cedar/Heinemann.
11 Psychosynthesis is a transpersonal therapy founded by Roberto Assagioli. See Assagioli, R., *Psychosynthesis: a manual of principles and techniques*, 1990 edn.; Wellingborough: Aquarian/Thorsons (first published 1965).

4 Every Day a Bonus

Vicki Harris

Vicki was only 36 at diagnosis in 1987, and the cancer had already spread to her ribs. After successful treatment, she continued to hold down a responsible job in a City company and also to bring up two children. In 1994 she had a recurrence of the disease, but is still optimistic. She took part in the television film *Cancer Positive* (1992) and also in *The Cancer War Story* (1995).

On the morning of Thursday 12 February 1987, one half of my brain was tackling some book-work at the set of barristers' chambers where I worked; the other half of my brain was instructing me to concentrate on an itch in my left breast. Neither side of the brain was paying much attention to either of the jobs in hand. Suddenly there it was: a lump the size of a pea, hard but painless. My up-until-now lethargic brain went into overdrive – any concentration flew out of the window.

I downed tools and somehow knew that I had to see my GP that night, and that's exactly what I did. By 5pm on Wednesday 18 February I had had cancer diagnosed and a mastectomy operation had been performed. Life would never be the same. In fact there's an advertisement on the television now that sums up my feelings at the time. It's the National Lottery advert where a huge index finger points through the window and a God-like voice says 'It's You'. That's how I felt – plucked from the crowd. I wasn't ill, I hadn't lost weight, my life was normal. I felt very lonely, but now I realise that I had joined the biggest club in the world, the Cancer Club: a club where class, money, sex, age, colour, religion – you name the barrier – simply doesn't exist.

The word 'cancer' obviously affects individuals differently, but the normal reaction is the thought of disease and death. I suppose I was no different in reacting that way, except that I was only 36 years old and still had that youthful illusion that death happens to other people, older people – not *you*! Looking back,

I suppose I was in a state of shock. I went with the flow. I didn't query anything or anyone. I had the operation and then a month of radiotherapy. I was well aware of alternative and complementary medicines but I never thought of either in place of orthodox treatment.

The only alternative that sprang to mind was the Bristol Cancer Help Centre. Before my illness I worked with a woman (who has since become my dear friend) who had had cancer some years before and had been to Bristol. She loaned me Penny Brohn's book *Gentle Giants*, which I read with interest. When I became ill, she and about seven or eight other people recommended that I get there soon, and therefore, after my radiotherapy, that was the next step.

Radiotherapy can be a very soul-destroying experience, and by the time I got to Bristol the initial shock, anxiety and sheer speed with which decisions were being taken had turned into a tearful depression. Therefore by the time my husband and I arrived at Bristol I think we both thought we were beyond repair, but we were quite wrong.

I don't know how to explain the atmosphere at Grove House, but an atmosphere there certainly is. It's like a pair of arms reaching out and gently drawing you in. There's a general feeling of comfort immediately you step inside, and above all no one looks at you with fear in their eyes. This was something I had great trouble in coping with in hospital. Perhaps it was my young age that made the nurses see me as a mirror image. Often they looked at me and didn't quite know how to react. They could so easily have been me. And my prognosis was poor: the disease had already spread to my ribs.

So my husband and I embarked on our week – a week that was to change our lives. As I said before, from the time of my diagnosis, operation and treatment I felt I had not made one decision regarding my future. I had been told – 'We'll take you down to the theatre' – 'Sign this form' – 'Don't worry about the drains in your chest; just routine' – 'We'll mark you out for radiotherapy' – and I just nodded. No one explained anything unless I asked, and sometimes the questions did not arrive at the correct time (often they came in the middle of the night), but at Bristol I was told everything I needed to know about my disease and treatment, and why mentally I was feeling the way I was. Best of all, I was told it doesn't have to be all doom and gloom. I had a future, and it was up to me to control it. I could change my diet; I could learn to meditate and put myself in a state of relaxation. I was taught to see potential stressful situations that I could control. I was back in the driving seat.

During my stay at Bristol I was approached by a couple of people who had sat in at our group sessions and was asked whether I would like to participate in research being sponsored by the Cancer Research Campaign (CRC) and the Imperial Cancer Research Fund (ICRF). I was told that the idea was to compare how women with breast cancer who went to Bristol fared, compared with women who didn't attend. I enthusiastically agreed; that was about mid-week by now. I knew that the more people with cancer knew about Bristol, the better the quality of life for those people would be. I was told that I would be sent questionnaires asking how I was progressing.

Well, eventually, and sadly, my week at Bristol was over, and I went home and put into practice the therapies that Bristol had shown me. Gradually my life became normal and confidence grew. I didn't think I had cancer every time I sneezed or had a pain in my big toe!

I totally forgot about the research project I had agreed to participate in, and only remembered when a questionnaire dropped on to the front doormat one morning. The questionnaire was straightforward. I just had to tick boxes in answer to specific questions, and there was a 'Further Comments' box at the end. By this time I was feeling fine, I was happy with my life, and for the first time I felt I had sorted out my priorities and was totally in control. I felt I owed all this to Bristol, and when I filled in the 'Further Comments' section I added another sheet of A4 to describe my much-improved quality of life.

In September 1990 one evening, going home, I bought, as usual, the *Evening Standard*, and there in big, black headlines I was informed that 'Positive thinking "won't cure cancer"'. I read on to discover that the survival of women who went to Bristol was 'significantly inferior' to that of women attending orthodox centres only. The next day the news was even worse: 'When the kind cure may kill' was the headline. Having never been a fan of the *Evening Standard* (it was just something to pass the time on the tube) I thought they had got their wires crossed; but I then realised they had received their information from a press release issued by the CRC and ICRF about a paper that was due to appear in the *Lancet* later that week. Here is the article.

When the kind cure may kill …
by Dr Myles Harris

The astonishing news that counselling, holistic medicine and spiritual support might make cancer worse seems scarcely credible. But it may be so.

In a report published tomorrow in the *Lancet* two groups of women suffering from breast cancer were compared. One group received the normal treatment – radiotherapy, surgery and drugs. The other received the standard treatment plus being offered attendance at the Bristol Cancer Help Centre. The centre, opened by the Prince of Wales seven years ago, offers patients counselling, spiritual and emotional support and treatments with diet, touch and holistic remedies. The disease-free survival of these women was, the report concludes, "significantly poorer" than those women who got the no-frills therapy.

While the youth of patients attending the centre may have been a factor, "It is certainly possible," concludes the report, "that the BCHC attenders may, in some subtle way, have worse diseases than our controlled series [*sic*], the possibility that some aspect of the centre's regimen may be responsible for their decreased survival must be faced."

Statistics are slippery things. I have on my desk a paper that shows Vitamin C to be marvellously beneficial in the treatment of cancer, and one, equally authoritatively, demonstrating that it is about as useful as a glass of cold water at the bottom of a swimming pool.

But not all statistics are wrong. The Bristol study was conducted by reputable people of good faith. It appears to be sound. It also shows a healthy respect for the truth by the centre that it offered to take part. If we are to assume what was found was true, it is important to speculate why.

Alternative medicine is, next to Islam, the fastest growing religion – albeit a secular one – in Britain. Counselling, a large element of alternative medicine, is a form of confessional capitalism, an idea that illness is caused by consumerism and can only be cured by a form of secular love from strangers called "caring".

There are counselling chapters in almost all towns. In London it supports an expensive PR organisation and no tragedy is ever enacted on TV without the reporter genuflecting to the need for the victims to be counselled. But if it becomes evident that such popularist support groups, however well-intentioned, can do harm, then we need to know quickly.

If the Bristol Cancer Help Centre adheres to the principles of the easy democracy of self-help and alternative medicine it will emphasise the informal. There will be none of the usual signs of a hospital; the clanking of trolleys, the mysterious, dimly frightening noises of crashing metal, the sweet sour medical smells or bowel-loosening signs to places like "Main Operating Theatre".

In alternative centres there will be no sisters in blue with clipboards, nor spotty medical students nor doctors waving terrifying looking X-rays. Instead the unit will be as much like home as possible.

The staff at such centres tend to be inflexibly informal, smiling people who insist on the use of Christian names. Elitist authority symbols such as "Doctor", "Nurse" or "Father", they will tell you, only serve to distance the patient.

How on earth could such inoffensive methods affect the progress of a tumour? One alarming possibility is that the centre quite inadvertently attracts people with a greater liability to die from cancer than normal. How could that be?

The answer may lie in the work of Professor Hans Eysenck and Grossarth-Maticek at the Institute of Psychiatry in London. They have controversially described personalities that are "overly cooperative, weak, unassertive, over-patient, defensive, harmony seeking and compliant ..." as particularly prone to cancer.

Studies of such people over 20 years suggest that they have a much higher incidence of cancer than aggressive or well-balanced personality types.

It is not unreasonable to speculate that this is where a flaw in the alternative treatment of cancer might lie. For holistic and "support" therapies, far from being radical alternatives to conventional treatment, are the essence of consumerist compliance. Instead of such therapies teaching the patient to get up and fight – Eysenck's categories of personality suggest that aggressive hostile people and well-adjusted people are many times less likely to get cancer – alternative medicine's emphasis on "nonconfrontational techniques" may teach the cancer victim to lie down and whisper comfortable phrases about "caring" or being "in touch with himself."

Such instructions may well send his natural killer cells, designed to destroy cancer, to sleep. Thus the poor prognosis.

This is unlikely to happen in a normal hospital. They are not meant to be frightening, but they inadvertently show you just enough of "the instruments" to make you aware of danger.

The figures from this study show that the fear-inspiring conventional hospital may have over the centuries evolved at least part of the correct mixture of order, rank and discipline to offer at least some hope of a cure. People are reassured by uniforms, stimulated by struggles and needled by fear. In the midst of such struggles they often discover who really among their relatives and friends loves them. In such lessons lie the roots of personality change.

Another alternative exists, but for it to happen it would mean the "carers" having to lie down with the psychological school of Professor Eysenck, a man whose wildly controversial work on race and intelligence and demolition of the idea that you can measure any effect from conventional psychotherapy (such therapy must, I believe, include a good deal of counselling and alternative medicine) rank him almost as the Beast of the Apocalypse in Left-wing eyes.

Eysenck of course is no beast, but a scientist before his time. His worse sin in caring eyes is his advocacy of behaviour therapy – a highly modified form of conditioning which involves learning to recognise and alter disabling personality traits. It has been used, successfully, to lower the risk of cancer in vulnerable groups, and improve prognosis in patients with cancer. Breast cancer patients on chemotherapy showed an increase in survival (over an average of 11.28 months) of 2.8 months. On behaviour therapy the increase was 3.64 months. Together the two treatments reinforced each other, resulting in a mean survival time of 22.4 months.

The holistic movement, if it has ignored such studies, cannot afford to do so any longer. Having had the courage to submit their work to ruthless scientific scrutiny they must now, like any other medical discipline, be willing to throw untested, well-meaning assumptions overboard in favour of facts. Eysenck may be their man.

Then the anger set in. What right had the researchers to publish such results after such a short time? Above all, I knew the results must be wrong. How can meditating, relaxing, receiving healing and counselling, and eating a healthy diet, kill anyone? Please pause here and think about this seriously – take time out to give it thought. Later on in this chapter you will read that the scientists of world-renowned establishments will not withdraw the research results. On what basis they refuse, I am at a total loss to understand, but more of this later – back to September 1990.

I was so angry at the article that when I got home I immediately wrote a letter to the *Evening Standard* expressing my view that the research must be wrong, and I criticised the NHS by saying that they took a very negative approach to cancer and its patients. I faxed the letter the next day – I was pleased with it and it was published that evening, with the *Standard*'s own heading:

A cancer in medical statistics

As I was one of the women involved in the Bristol Cancer Help Centre mentioned by Dr Myles Harris (When the kind cure may kill, 6 September) I would like to put the other side of the story.

I attended Bristol in April 1987 at the age of 37 having undergone a mastectomy and radiotherapy treatment for breast cancer. The centre puts the patient back in control, something that the negative attitudes of doctors and nurses cannot do. (I even comforted a crying nurse who became upset when hearing of my poor prognosis.)

Bristol does not have magic cures, nor does it promise to extend life span, but it does give one the opportunity to reassess the situation, release any old emotions and help the patient face prospective death as positively as possible.

Emotions obviously run high, but if the media knew what damage is done to patients by surveys and statistics that don't give the full story then I am sure reporting would be handled with more care.

Over the past three years, through connections with Bristol, I have met many people with cancer, some of whom have died, but they died by their rules, being able (thanks to the teachings of Bristol) to go with no guilt and the ability to look loved ones in the eye to say goodbye. How can this be so badly criticised? – Vicki Harris.

There were several other letters published in various newspapers, written by other women who had taken part in the research, over the next few weeks.

Six weeks later I attended my hospital for my routine six-monthly check with my consultant. I stripped to the waist and lay on his couch, and he started to examine me. I don't think in the years I'd been seeing him he ever looked me in the eye; he was a cold character, but he was totally different this time. While pinning me to the table, on the pretence of taking my pulse (something he had never done before) he asked me whether it had been me who had written to the *Evening Standard*. I smiled, feeling pleased with myself that he was showing an interest, and replied 'Yes'. Well, all hell was let loose. He said his name was well known in political circles and that was where he was receiving flak from regarding my letter. (I must point out that in the letter I made no reference to the hospital where I had received my treatment.) How had anyone associated me to that consultant and that hospital? Had anyone looked at my medical records without my permission? My consultant was furious. If I had had a lump the size of an orange he would never have found it. The examination was a sham. I was lost for words, and never put up an argument at the time. I had entered his room prepared for a routine examination; instead I got an interrogation. As I left his room he called after me that I would live for a good few years yet: I think I detected a note of disappointment in his voice.

It was only when I got home that I realised how distressed I was. He had got me at my most vulnerable. A woman exposing her breasts and being examined is normally embarrassed to a degree. It's even more embarrassing when there's only one boob! In fact a friend of mine said I ought to have asked him to remove his trousers and pants so we could have the discussion on a more equal footing.

I resolved to change hospitals and consultant, but being a Taurean I'm lazy, and never got around to it during the following six months. After that time I returned for another routine examination. I had recently returned from a holiday in the USA and was looking well. The change in my consultant was amazing. He asked me (looking me in the eye) where I had been to get such a tan, why I hadn't sent him a postcard and how long I had worked for barristers (I'd never told him where I worked). I answered his questions politely, had my examination and went to leave when

I glanced at my notes, and there at the top, underlined in red, were the words 'legal profession'. I left his room immediately, went to my GP and got referral letters to another hospital. I have never seen, nor wish to see, that consultant again. I find it hard to understand how I had received such treatment and investigation just because I had defended the Bristol Centre in my letter to the *Standard*. What are 'they' frightened of?

Well, that was the effect the research had on me personally, but the effect it had on Bristol was much more deep-rooted and long-lasting. The administration, the therapists, in fact everyone at Bristol, were devastated. Television appearances and interviews were given, and Bristol appeared to be digging themselves in deeper and deeper.

I could not understand why people at the Centre were responding to the media in the way they were. In my heart of hearts I knew that the research was flawed, and yet here was Bristol back-tracking on its methods and therapies. They were questioning themselves, something I never dreamt of doing. Bristol had taught us to have faith in ourselves and our abilities. Why were they so worried? I was angry that they had lost faith in themselves. Overnight their waiting list had disappeared, money was drying up and their reputation was seriously dented. So why did they not take a firm stand and defend themselves, instead of acting remorsefully? It was a learning experience for both Bristol and its clients.

During this time I was approached by Heather Goodare, a fellow participant in the Bristol survey. She was trying to form a group from the women who had agreed to take part in the research and who were prepared to give up some spare time to support Bristol in any way they could. I was only too willing to help and gradually we formed the Bristol Survey Support Group, meeting monthly at St James's Church, Piccadilly, to gather ideas and suggestions to help Bristol.

As a group we realised that the research had fundamental problems. Like was not compared to like, and many factors had not been taken into account. For instance, some women at Bristol had more advanced tumours than the control group. No account had been taken of the quality of life of the Bristol participants. Men and women often go to Bristol as a last resort rather than an early alternative and are therefore more ill, as proved to be the case here.

While the Group was gathering information, the researchers admitted that the research was flawed, but they flatly refused to withdraw it. Again, I ask you to think carefully about this. How can such gentle therapies be harmful – how can they kill – how can they be detrimental? What are the big boys afraid of?

The few allies that cancer sufferers have are the researchers. This is where our hope lies, and yet here were the two biggest funding bodies scaring patients and (it seemed to us) trying to put a stop to other patients enjoying Bristol's programme for a better quality of life in the future. Why? Perhaps research money is involved – I mean, where would the drug companies be if it was found that Bristol's therapies prolonged life just as well as hard chemotherapy drugs?

Our group then started down the track to get the rules of research changed. Never should a group of people who willingly participate in research be put through so much distress. It seems that once you agree to help, you lose all human identity and become a number, faceless and emotionless. We should have been informed about the outcome of the survey, and been given the opportunity to challenge it, before it was published and did so much damage.

Well, it is now five years on from the initial research and eight years on from my diagnosis. Bristol remains in trouble. Major reorganisation has been carried out – and a lot of self-examination and soul-searching. Attendance has increased, but they are still a long way off their pre-research figures. I feel things would improve there if the survey report were withdrawn in a reasonable blaze of publicity. Unless that happens, sadly, many people will never receive the benefits that I and many thousands of other cancer patients have had; but, as I have mentioned before, the big boys won't allow that to happen, for reasons that only they will ever know. I can only imagine that they never relax on a bed and meditate, in case it kills them.

I have had an eventful few years. I have been diagnosed with damage to the brachial plexus of my left arm, due to overdosage of radiotherapy at the time of my mastectomy. I am now registered disabled and have had to give up my job. Of course the medical profession are having trouble admitting it might be their fault.

In the past year I have also had a recurrence of cancer confirmed. I was extremely sick in the summer of 1994 and eventually went back to my dreaded local hospital at 1 o'clock one Tuesday morning in August, as an emergency. I was left on a trolley, vomiting, for eight hours; was looked at by a junior doctor; and was eventually sent home with a bottle of Aludrox (an antacid used to treat indigestion) and told I would receive an out-patient consultant's appointment shortly. Even with my history I was not kept in for observation. By Thursday of that week I used my private patient's healthcare plan and admitted myself to a private hospital. Within a week I had cancer diagnosed and began chemotherapy treatment. Two weeks later I received an out-patient's appointment from my local hospital for October – two months later. I felt it was likely that I would have died by then.

So you see, the NHS has really let me down. Through orthodox treatment I am disabled, and without private treatment I would be dead, but thanks to the Bristol programme and my attitude to life I live to fight another day.

There was a time when I would never have participated in private treatment, but I was left with no choice. I thought it was queue-jumping but now realise there is more involved. I receive treatment that is not readily available on the NHS. I take anti-sickness pills that the NHS will not purchase because of the expense. I receive a blood test that measures my active cancer cells, which would not be noticed, if I was an NHS patient, until another lump appeared. What a sorry state of affairs!

Cancer has changed my life and my opinions. If anything it has improved my quality of life, in spite of all I have been through. Every day is a bonus, as indeed it should be for all of us, but sometimes it takes an illness or a tragedy for us to recognise the fact. Sadly, many of you will join the Club, but remember it can be the beginning and not the end.

5 Canada is my Homeland

Sumi Jenner

Sumi is Japanese Canadian, married to an Englishman, and still working hard in their joint management consultancy business. She was 52 when her cancer was diagnosed in 1987, at a time when the Canadian government was making amends for the wartime internment of Japanese Canadians.

The telephone was ringing.

It was my brother, calling from Toronto, Canada. The one I had come to see on a two-week visit to London. I stayed on, and that was 30 years ago.

I gripped the telephone and steeled myself for bad news, as in those days a long-distance call at that time of night could mean just that. The news, however, was that the Canadian government had apologised and agreed to redress each and every Japanese Canadian interned during the Second World War. A sum of money would be paid as well. I was one of them, an interned Canadian child.

In the months to follow, my mind was in a constant spin: the years in the internment camp and the release and relief when the war ended; the years of racism and hate which I never fully understood. Canada is my homeland, not Japan: why had they put our family in jail? All this past history tossed around in my head, all mixed up with the present – my children verging on their teenage years, our business of managing musicians which my husband Peter and I operated from our home, overtaking our house and lives.

My head whizzed around and around, and I felt it in my body as well. I knew I was not well: three different doctors gave me three different diagnoses. I was working late, eating badly and smoking like a chimney. Peter was away a lot, touring with Billy Bragg in Europe and the Soviet Union.

Deep down, I just wanted to run away from my life. After all, I now had money of my own, more than I had ever had. It was possible: but where to go, what about the children? I couldn't leave them, ever. I felt trapped, a prisoner in the house.

Then I discovered the lump in my right breast. It was very small and I was not afraid, then. It was early spring in 1987, usually my best time of the year.

Things happened very quickly after that. I went to see a female 'breast specialist', recommended by my GP, and was told, yes, there is a lump. I already knew this. I was to go into hospital a week later for a 'test'. No other information was offered, and my trust in the medical profession was never in question. A friend had had a lump in her breast which turned out to be non-malignant.

There were five other women admitted into the ward on the day I went into hospital; new arrivals like me. A certain air of camaraderie prevailed, as we got to know each other, giving our reasons for being there. I felt no fear and being in a women-only situation was very comforting, strangers though they were.

When I came to after the 'test', I looked around and the five other girls were gone, their beds stripped. I saw there were plastic jars draped above my waist and I knew something was wrong. My first reaction was that I knew how and why I got to this and I was going to find my way back! This remained vivid in my mind for many, many months.

Cancer was a word never uttered in the ward. I had to ask and ask I did of everyone bar the patients on the ward, and finally I was told by the intern. I felt no emotion but this soon turned to disbelief and anger when I learnt that while under general anaesthetic, a biopsy was taken, the lump removed and a good strong dose of chemotherapy injected, with no warning and no counselling (before or after).

And of course, my hair started to fall out. This was the only visible sign of the disease to me, and I became very frightened. The lump, now removed, had been so little. What was this cancer thing? My father had died with stomach cancer, as did so many of his friends. Cancer only happened to older people, I thought. Does this mean I am to die at only 52 years of age?

The protocol then was six weeks of chemotherapy, followed by the same period of radiotherapy. Was it six months or six weeks of each? I cannot now remember, only that it was a most frightening prospect at the time.

I wanted a week's holiday to consider undergoing all this, but this was flatly refused. 'No, no, no, that is not in the protocol,' was the answer. At this point Peter and I walked out of the doctor's office. She was too busy even to look up at us during our very brief 'consultation'. We had waited more than two hours to see her. I learnt later, too, that the hospital I attended is known as 'the butcher's table' in certain medical circles.

One of our clients, Hank Wangford, who had become a friend, talked to me about the Bristol Cancer Help Centre and holistic medicine. Peter made an appointment for me to see a homoeopathic GP, recommended by Hank. The doctor also mentioned Bristol, as well as the Royal Marsden Hospital: the hospital for cancer cases.

I was very wary and suspicious of everything at that point, but Peter made all the arrangements for us to go to Bristol together. 'They sound so warm and caring on the telephone,' he said. Indeed, the warm welcome we received at the Centre and the caring atmosphere there was in sharp contrast to the bleak Victorian surrounds of the hospital where I had had my lump removed. It was like going from a human body factory to a country house of kind and gentle friends.

Meeting the various members of the staff and the other participants that day changed my entire outlook on life and, probably, Peter's. There was a quiet, vibrant atmosphere.

Cancer was not a 'shhhh word' but, rather, discussed openly. My first experience with a spiritual healer that afternoon was profound. Few words were spoken, nothing seemed to be happening, but at the end of the session, a flood of tears came – the first time I had wept since my diagnosis – and then, peace.

We came home exhausted. I read everything I could about cancer. I also read Penny Brohn's book *Gentle Giants*, over and over again. Peter read all the academic stuff and statistics – we combed the bookshop shelves for even more information. We bored our friends and wellwishers rigid with the information we had acquired.

It took some time to get the appointment at the Royal Marsden Hospital. Once there, the gentle doctor's first words were: 'How can I help you?' He gave me much encouragement and support, listening carefully as I went through my recent experiences at the hospital and my visit to the Bristol Centre. Never was there any pressure from him for me to undertake any conventional therapy. He kindly arranged to monitor my progress through the Bristol way with regular examinations and tests. He also suggested a course of the anti-oestrogen drug, tamoxifen, which I agreed to.

There were many ups and a lot more downs, going backwards, and angry, angry words initially. Recovery from the effects of the chemotherapy took months. I learnt later that the dosage was much too much for me. In those days, they did not tailor the dose to suit the patient's needs – it was the belt and braces treatment. I understand this is done much more sympathetically now, in small doses, and with a much more consultative, rather than authoritarian approach.

The change to a vegetarian diet was an enormous U-turn, but luckily Peter and the children went along with it. They had no choice, really, as I was completely obsessed with my recovery programme. I was determined to find my way back and could not identify with the hopeless/helpless patient.

I take all the vitamins as recommended by the Bristol Centre: this is an important part of their programme for me. There is the odd day when I forget to take the supplements, and the lack of energy is noticeable.

At first, I made small changes in my lifestyle and it helped to make the bigger changes easier, later. I found a Japanese shiatsu masseuse who was marvellous. She came every week for a year and made me aware of my body and the need to breathe properly.

I joined a healing circle and went to that every week, learning to visualise, which I found difficult to do on my own. I devised an exercise programme at home and do a half-hour every morning. I listened to Matthew Manning (a gifted healer), then went to one of his seminars. And learnt to relax and live with cancer.

I read Lawrence LeShan's books, and still read his book on meditation, and practise at least once a day. I went to the Centre twice to hear him speak. He has a warm sense of humour and made me laugh for the first time in months. I look forward to when I can see and hear Bernie Siegel speak. [Dr Siegel is an American surgeon who has written several books for and about cancer patients. From time to time he visits the UK.]

My first acupuncture experience was not good, so it was some months before I took up a friend's recommendation to see her acupuncturist. This practitioner turned out to be extremely well qualified, warm and caring, and her manner was of someone who considered it a personal challenge to get me going again. How could I not get better with someone like that to look after me? I see her at least once a month.

Injections of Iscador (a mistletoe extract) were recommended by my homoeopathic GP and eventually I learnt to inject myself, overcoming my queasiness about needles. These injections did me much good, helping me to open out and see life in a different light.

In the autumn of that first year, my lump returned and it grew and grew to the size of a walnut. It was certainly bigger than the first one. Although it is not unusual to have a second growth, it was disheartening. I eventually evolved an exercise in visualisation, calling on all my favourite male film stars. They all wore white overalls, with my name on the back, and everyone I asked turned up. Peter was also there, ushering them in through a narrow porthole. Marlon Brando would always take a little time squeezing through the small opening. Down the chute they would slide, down to a giant walnut. They would then set about scrubbing and brushing until the walnut became invisible.

My faith in the Bristol programme remains unshaken. I still have that lump and, with visualisation, plenty of rest and all the rest of the programme, it has reduced somewhat. Perhaps only scar tissue remains.

I am now in my ninth year of living with cancer. At least once a day I think of my lump getting smaller and I talk to it. It is like a barometer in my body: it gets hard and angry when I am doing too much. It is soft and pliant when I am relaxed. I am no longer on tamoxifen, as it was not doing anything for me except to make me retain water and generally cause discomfort.

I have been back to Vancouver, Canada for a reunion, 50 years on, with all the other wartime internees. There were 6,000 of us, survivors all. I saw the beauty of the city, something which I had not known. We were taken on a tour of the islands, paid visits to cemeteries, among them a cemetery of Japanese Canadian veterans who fought for Canada in the war, and caught up with each other's lives. One subject matter was the redress money and what each of us did or was planning to do with it. During the course of that wonderful week, my brothers, my sister and I stood together again on the street where we were all born. It had taken us 50 years.

We had moved on eastward from the camp after the war ended, finally stopping in Montreal, as friends of the family found lodgings for us. I lived in Montreal for over ten years. My final stop, however, was London, on that famous holiday. Here, I thought I could shut the door on a scarred childhood.

I am grateful to the Canadian government for making my recovery possible. I would have found it very difficult without the financial resources. The letter of apology signed by the prime minister hangs in the bedroom.

I am thankful to my husband Peter for his loving support. There were times when I wondered which of us had the cancer. He was totally committed to helping me recover.

I am thankful to Heather Goodare for inviting me to write a chapter for this book, and gently prodding me on. She had asked over a year ago, but I realised that the process of looking back was not something I could do easily. I was very reluctant, but having to write everything down like this has reinforced my beliefs in the Bristol Centre's teachings and, in a way, in myself.

I have been back to the Centre several times since that first visit. There have been changes there, new ideas, new people, but my faith in their philosophy and what it means to me remains unchanged. I shall be grateful to the Centre for the rest of my life.

6 Threads of Many Colours

Sigyn Roberts

Sigyn, of Swedish origin, born in 1935, married an Englishman, Glyn, who has used many of her personal papers to add to his own memories of her. Sigyn's cancer was already advanced when it was diagnosed in 1987. She worked as a teacher until shortly before her death in June 1994.

Introduction by Sigyn's husband, Glyn

Sigyn was born in a woodcutter's cottage in Sweden. Her maiden name Ärlig means 'honest' and it fitted her character well. She radiated openness and kindness. Sigyn did some teaching and volunteer service in France and Africa before we met and married in Paris. After a spell in Ethiopia, we set up home in Sweden, but in the early 1970s we moved with our two sons to England. The move was very much against her wishes and during our early years here she felt quite lonely and at a loss. This was made worse by my own job, launching and running a Third World charity, which dominated our lives for several years and often took me away from home. But with the birth of a third son, with some part-time jobs and improving our old house on the edge of the Solent, she began to feel more at home. And when in 1986 she pipped 40 other candidates to gain a full-time English teaching post, life seemed wonderful.

In January 1987 Sigyn discovered a lump in her right breast. She reported it to her GP and was informed – following an external examination and mammography – that it was benign. During the following months it continued to grow, and the breast became massively misshapen. She made repeated requests for investigation and was told, among other things, 'not to be hysterical'. Finally, in December 1987 she managed to insist on a needle biopsy and learnt a week later that she had inoperable breast cancer. The consultant who had managed her case for almost a year advised radiotherapy 'and Valium, if that will make you feel any better' [sic].

She and I made two day visits to the Bristol Cancer Help Centre and Sigyn took to the complementary therapies with great enthusiasm, though six months of chewing raw vegetables proved a strain on her digestive tract. She also went through 50 sessions of radiotherapy and didn't find them too difficult physically, though the hospital setting was often depressing. At least she had confidence in the female head of radiotherapy. Whether it was the radiotherapy or the Bristol regime, her primary tumour had completely disappeared by June and even the scar tissue had gone, to the surprise of the radiotherapy staff. Sigyn was jubilant, though she still attended quarterly check-ups.

Nevertheless, she felt she had been grossly neglected by the earlier lack of diagnosis and treatment. For several months she wrote and telephoned all manner of authorities to request an inquiry. Time and again, her letters and telephone calls led nowhere, and obstacles were put in her way, but she persisted with resolve. After 18 months, thanks to some prodding by the local Community Health Council (CHC), a formal hearing was called. This involved senior medical advisers from around the country, and the GP and consultant who had previously been responsible for her care.

The hearing found Sigyn's complaints fully justified, which pleased her. A letter from the Community Health Council later commented:

There is no doubt, so far as the CHC is concerned, that you have done a good deed for the people in this health district by taking the trouble and enduring the stress of having your case investigated in order to highlight shortfalls and failures in existing services.

But at the end of the day, she told me, all Sigyn had really wanted was for the doctors concerned to come across the room to her and say they were sorry. They never did.

In May 1991 her quarterly check-up brought devastating news: secondaries had developed. Somehow this was even more shattering than the earlier blow. Sigyn went through radiotherapy again, having far less, as she had already neared her maximum dose, but found it more painful the second time round. She took the mistletoe extract Iscador prescribed by a new and sympathetic GP and made many visits to the Royal Homoeopathic Hospital. She also embarked with enthusiasm on the Gerson therapy, which required organic vegetable juices, coffee enemas, a self-hypnosis video and much else. She had friendly advice in this from the Debra Stappard Trust (which supports people on the Gerson therapy), and gained much encouragement from members of the Bristol Survey Support Group in London, whom she admired for their campaign to question and have withdrawn some very 'anti-Bristol' findings by the ICR research team. A weekly visit to a warm and gentle healer also brought Sigyn extra strength, and to some extent these sessions helped her come to terms with mortality.

Besides keeping a lovely home overlooking the water and caring for our family, Sigyn continued to work at what she especially enjoyed, teaching English as a second language. Her students were mostly immigrants detained at a local prison. She also taught art and textiles and took special pleasure in working with detainees from many different cultures to produce good-quality handicraft. Several of their joint efforts won prizes in the annual Arthur Koestler competitions for artwork by people in prison.

Sigyn was always full of kindness, life and enthusiasm – cycling everywhere, visiting friends, keeping up the allotment, cooking delicious meals. But she also dared to stand up for what she believed, particularly in justice for the Third World and for the dignity and self-respect of the detainees with whom she worked. Somehow, she managed to combine her kindness and her solidarity, so that she was both loved and respected.

But her pain and disability increased during 1993, even though we never really knew what was cancer and what was arthritis. In December, her health finally collapsed. Sigyn refused chemotherapy and struggled on for six months in increasing pain, but died at home with her family around her on 28 June 1994. The boys (now young men) and I miss her terribly, as do her numerous friends, 200 of whom came to her funeral.

The following are extracts from essays that Sigyn wrote for a counselling course in 1990. They reveal some of the inner stresses that she felt despite her outward cheerfulness. I should emphasise that she was never anti-English, though she criticised aspects of life here – and usually with good reason.

Sigyn's story

I was brought up in a large family in Sweden, non-intellectual and materially poor. The Lutheran work ethic dominated. To do one's duty, to be helpful and honest, were considered most important. Boastfulness was a mortal sin. The Swedish equivalents of the terms 'self-assured' or 'self-confident' had a definite negative ring to them. I am sure this attitude, though later modified, played an important role in my life.

I studied to become a junior school teacher, yet the values continued much the same. My horizons didn't widen much, but as I became financially more independent I began to travel, taking jobs in places as varied as Lapland, Paris and Nigeria. I now met people with other beliefs and values. This excited and confused me as I began to realise how complex the world was.

I also fell seriously in love. My British husband and I moved to Ethiopia, working with the Swedish overseas aid programme, but after 18 months we resigned and returned to Sweden. We felt that European countries and the USA were carrying out colonial approaches in their aid programmes. This was perhaps the first time I had challenged authority.

Next, we set off to sail round the world with two friends. I don't really like sailing but went along to please my husband. On the Isle of Wight, I was relieved to find that I was pregnant, so I went back to Gothenburg, picked up a teaching job and let the others cross the Atlantic.

The next 20 years have been centred round our three children. I felt that I should do everything I could to give them a happy and stable childhood and a good start in life. Our first years as parents were in Gothenburg, where my husband taught sociology at the university and I was a housewife. My husband, though a good family man in his way, also had other expectations beyond carrying on with work and family responsibilities. Sweden seemed too well organised for him to be needed there. We moved to England, where he did research into social services and later set up a Third World charity.

I had thought of myself as very adaptable and believed I could live happily anywhere. It came as a shock to me to realise how ill at ease and unhappy I felt living in England. Our eldest son, who had been a happy and placid child, became difficult. All sorts of facilities for children – crèches, special facilities on trains and buses, things that I had taken for granted at home – were lacking. What I did find were damp houses, foods full of additives, streets full of litter and dog dirt, lead in the water, air pollution … I just wanted to run away! I had no feeling of belonging, other than to my family.

The class system struck me as grotesque and I found it difficult to find friends. What I saw of British society I couldn't understand or appreciate: so much competitiveness, so little cooperation, so many drop-outs. Those who could get on, did very nicely, but at the same time many led miserable lives. It is my experience that most foreigners become immediately aware of the system when they arrive here. It seems to permeate every facet of life – schooling, housing, health, social life – yet when I talk about it to English people, they often seem to think that it does not exist. The situation hasn't changed much over the years. I have just had to close my eyes to it, otherwise I would have been angry most of the time.

There is a lot of ignorance and sometimes prejudice here about the non-English. It is surprising how many people confuse Sweden and Switzerland. 'Do you have cuckoo clocks and high mountains where you come from? ... Oh, from *Sweden* ... Shouldn't you be blonde with blue eyes? What about blue movies and free love then? Why do so many of you commit suicide?' (Perhaps Sweden did top that list some time in the 1950s, but several other countries now have higher rates.)

Even though I could speak English fluently, my accent meant that I was recognised as a foreigner as soon as I opened my mouth. People would then respond in different ways. Some seemed confused, some raised their voices, others would talk painfully slowly. Pace is certainly important – we need to speak clearly and slowly to those who are new to a language – but it can be quite insulting to be talked to as if you are brain-damaged or deaf, or both, when in fact you understand as well as the next person.

It was also insulting when I went to see a doctor for the first time in England. My husband had gone with me, not as an interpreter, but to help me find my way around. I told the doctor of my complaint and he considered it for a little while before writing a prescription and turning to my husband. 'She should take this twice a day ...' I was totally bypassed, though he must have known that I could understand perfectly well. This hit me as a *loss of dignity*.

When you speak in a foreign language, you often can't express yourself with quite the same precision or use quite the same nuances as when you use your own language. Sometimes you actually end up saying something you do not want to say. This, I find, leads to a *loss of confidence*.

As you are often perceived according to your language ability, linguistic problems can create frustration and *loss of identity*. I had a good example of this in class the other day. We were doing a simple exercise – something like *-s* in the third person singular – when an Egyptian student who was struggling with the concept threw down his pen, pounded the table and said, 'I am *not* stupid, I'm not silly. I'm writing a book at home. I know Beethoven, Bach, Goethe ....' I understood, but can English people fully know this feeling?

Another difficult area is humour. This varies from culture to culture. Many jokes depend on plays on words which need a good command of the language. Even if you understand, you might not be able to respond in kind quickly. A lot of humour, too, depends on the taboos of a culture. While I've been in England, comedians like the Two Ronnies and Benny Hill have been very popular. Their stock is largely innuendo about 'bottoms and boobs', and it seems that any comedian can dissolve a British audience simply be saying the word 'knickers'. If Swedes don't find clothing or parts of the body especially funny, I don't think it's because 'they have no sense of humour'.

Another kind of humour, very prevalent in English comedy programmes, is the parodying of foreign accents: Indian, German, Swedish ... I discussed this with a group of students recently. We agreed that while it might be funny in small doses, it can become quite insulting when done to excess.

Generally speaking, I feel that by moving to a foreign country I have lost something of my identity. When I got married I parted with my maiden name and so in some measure lost a bit of myself. When I meet people in England and tell them my first name, they sometimes respond, '*Sigyn*?? Well that's a nice name, but, ah, *difficult*! I'll call you Cindy (or Sibyl, or Sigrid).' If only English people could imagine what it might be like for them ('*Richard* – that's a difficult name. We'll call you Rajiv.'). With this sort of reaction when I first meet people, it's not surprising that I sometimes feel inhibited.

Then there's the question of standards. Swedes are very concerned with good health, ecology, food safety and such. The discussions we have recently seen in England had mostly taken place in Sweden 20 years ago, before we left. I was really disappointed in the early years to find that foodstuffs here often had no declaration of contents, and if there was one, the list of additives was frightening. There were masses of inferior and harmful food products on the supermarket shelves.

There were good ones too, but it was quite a job to find which was which, and even harder to persuade unwilling children to avoid lurid-coloured drinks, chalk-coloured bread and poisonous-looking jellies. Additives like tartrazine had been banned long ago in Sweden. When I used to ask for washing powders that did not contain phosphates, the shop assistants would look at me as if I was out of my mind.

That was 15 to 20 years ago now and much has improved, but for years these things seemed very important to me, especially as we had children. I was often ridiculed because of my worrying, and this in turn led to more worry and frustration.

But even today different cultural values can cause trouble. Let's take honesty versus politeness. One of our children had a stomach upset a while back. Our kindly neighbour, chatting to me over the garden fence, offered a bottle of medicine for my son. The medicine was prescribed. I said 'No, thanks,' and told her that I thought sharing prescribed medicines was not a good idea. When my husband heard about this he said, 'Why make such a meal of it? You could have just taken the bottle, put it in the cupboard for a few days and returned it with thanks when Daniel had recovered.' We clearly had different priorities. As an Englishman he was concerned with politeness; as a Swede I felt that I should be honest.

You will have noticed that I have used terms like: loss of confidence, loss of dignity, loss of identity … words like ill at ease, worried, insulted. It is not surprising that such feelings, often in combination with other things, such as lack of job opportunities and loss of contact with family and friends in one's own country, can lead to isolation, unhappiness, depression or even physical illness.

As I am ending here, may I just say that I have chosen to emphasise the problems. Of course there are many positive aspects to English society and I have found most people friendly and welcoming.

Postscript by Glyn Roberts

I feel that the extracts above, though instructive, leave a rather negative feel that is quite unfair to Sigyn. Friends who contacted me after her death mentioned the privilege it had been to know such a brave and lovely person. One wrote, 'I remember the first time I met her thinking what a wonderful woman Glyn's wife was. Such an open, smiling face, such beautiful eyes, that gorgeous Swedish lilt in her voice and her sweet-tempered patience with Glyn's obsession.'

Sigyn was rare and precious in many ways, and laughing at herself was a quality that we all admired and cherished in her. It released her to be who she wanted to be, and she was good at so many things.

A friend with advanced multiple sclerosis told me:

I would like to cope as well with my illness as she coped with hers. Besides those qualities that one would admire in anyone in that situation – courage, humour, determination – an extraordinary beauty emanated from her. She helped me come to terms with mortality. Some will have lived longer, but few will have lived and died with such grace.

Others stressed her qualities as a teacher. Colleagues remembered the fun and laughter, and recalled that they too had learnt from her: about the joy of drawing the best out of someone, when to be sympathetic and when to be firm.

Besides letters, we received a number of poems. Several implied that she had not really died, but was merely waiting somewhere else: death was an illusion. These messages were very kindly meant, but however comforting I could not honestly believe them. Then some lines came from a friend, Peter McDermott, who had just lost his own father. Although a Christian, Peter did not try to raise any expectations of a future life or reunion, but simply described how it felt to lose someone very dear.

Threads

When the fabric is torn
pulled apart by life or by death
the better the weaving
with many threads criss-crossing
holding together and
making a pleasing pattern
with their many colours

the better the weaving
the more ugly and painful
the gaping hole

The more threads
the longer it takes
to find their broken ends
to weave them back
to make some sense
and understanding from them

So mending
so healing can come
and the threads be used in some new pattern
that has woven into it
the precious memory of
what is missing

7 Me: Why Me?*

Hilary Scott

Hilary was aged 38 when her cancer was diagnosed in 1986. She was the first to respond to Heather's request to write her story, and completed it in 1991, shortly before her death in 1992.

There was no premonition that this day would dramatically change the rest of my life. I found a walnut-sized lump in my left breast, and so began the course of events which continue, after six years, to test my strength and courage beyond what I believed possible.

'You have a growth', pronounced the surgeon, bending over me as I lay on the paper-covered hospital examining table. It seemed an obvious remark. My question sounded casual: 'Do you mean a malignant growth?' I don't know how I expected him to reply, but I didn't think he would be so sure when he said that in his opinion it was malignant.

(Somewhere, in the back of my mind, though, the diagnosis seemed inevitable. I had often felt that cancer would be my fate; my mother had died of it in her late forties.)

So this is what it feels like to be told you have cancer. Shock, numbness, fear, unreality – this can't actually be happening to *me*.

The actual word cancer had been carefully avoided – something I have found over the years to be a very common omission. So much so, that when my daughter and I recently saw a genetic counsellor and every other word he said was 'cancer', or 'breast cancer', we got the giggles, as it has become a standing joke to talk of oncology, disease, tumour, but not *the* dreaded word!

A friend had told me the previous day that nine out of ten lumps are benign, but I thought, cynically at the time, someone has to be the unlucky one. And now it appeared to be me. The surgeon

* An abridged version of this chapter originally appeared in Barraclough, J. (ed.), *Cancer and Emotion: a practical guide to psycho-oncology*, 2nd edn, 1993; Chichester: Wiley.

explained to me and my husband that he planned a segmental mastectomy, to remove a wedge of my left breast, and that the operation would be followed by a course of radiotherapy, as a safety measure, to destroy any cancer cells left behind.

It was January 1986, and he advised taking until Easter off from my job as a playgroup supervisor. Suddenly I was out of control of my life; cancer had invaded my body and terror was fast invading my mind.

And so it all began: my long battle with cancer. But for years I had been fighting another battle against the insidious depression, anxiety and panic which frequently engulfed me. Many, many times all I wanted to do was to give up on everything, shrink into oblivion and find peace – death seemed the only way to be free. And now I had come face to face with death. The experience of cancer has changed my life.

When I began to read all I could about breast cancer, in early 1986, I discovered that I appeared to fit almost too perfectly into the typical 'cancer personality'. I had suffered from anxiety and depression since the age of eleven. I had been hospitalised on numerous occasions, seen various psychiatrists, taken literally hundreds of anti-depressants and tranquillisers, all in an attempt to put to flight the huge black bird which so often seemed to be perching on my shoulder, causing total despair and several suicide attempts. I was completely at odds with the world. I found relationships very difficult as I was constantly afraid of rejection; I suffered severe panic attacks, which for years prevented me from going out and about and leading a normal life. Life was a continual struggle: I felt totally inadequate and unsatisfied with everything. So when I was diagnosed as having breast cancer, this is how I was: unhappy, anxious, insecure.

I had a normal, happy childhood up until the age of eleven, when something went drastically wrong. The beginning of my problems seems to date from a seemingly trivial incident, when my best friend falsely accused me, behind my back to other friends at school, of stealing from her. The matter was cleared up, but not without our parents being involved and the headmistress making an issue of it in assembly. It is only as I write this that this event seems to be the obvious cause of my subsequent problems of anxiety, panic attacks and a deep-rooted fear of rejection.

I began to be reluctant to go to school (by this time I had passed the 11-plus and changed schools, so was no longer with the girl who had hurt me) and suffered from claustrophobia, especially in school assemblies. I have no recollection of the incident at assembly where my friend was made to apologise to me publicly, but that lack of memory in itself seems significant.

The result of all this was that I ended up in hospital. The next months of my life seemed to take on a nightmare quality. The psychiatrist treating me told my parents not to visit me for two or three weeks. Although they initially agreed to this, they subsequently tried to see me but were not allowed. Meanwhile I was undergoing narcosis – sleep treatment, so that I was drugged and each time I awoke I was drugged again. Often I resisted – I wouldn't drink the paraldehyde, so it had to be injected. It was not explained to me why my parents didn't visit. I was abandoned, alone, rejected and very frightened. Around me the majority of the other children were epileptic. I didn't understand what was happening to me, or why.

Was I like them – did I have fits? Was I mad? I emerged as an anxious, insecure twelve-year-old, believing that my parents had deliberately deserted me for those vital weeks, and questioning that they were actually my true parents. After all, how could loving parents have subjected an eleven-year-old to what I had been through? Medicines and injections forced on me; no explanation.

An incident I remember particularly was when a nurse insisted that I had a bath. I refused and so was picked up screaming and kicking and dumped in the bath in my nightdress – a new nightdress which my mother had made for me.

So, in this state I was sent, on medical advice, to a boarding school just before my thirteenth birthday. The school was an Anglican convent and after initial difficulties I settled down and spent five very happy years there. I did quite well academically but, more importantly, found security and healing.

The basis of my Christian faith was sown at school; a faith which has wavered considerably over the years, but which has never left me completely. I was a keen Girl Guide and gained my Queen's Guide award, a boost to my confidence. I still had difficulty with relationships, and I was frequently overdemanding of my friends. I gained a place at Whitelands College and went there in 1966 to do teacher training.

But the change brought all the old insecurities flooding back, and I had to leave in the summer, on the point of a breakdown. The next year or so was difficult and filled with significant emotional events. I split up with a boyfriend of two years' standing; my mother was ill and underwent a hysterectomy. She died suddenly while I was away for a weekend. This experience influenced the way I approached my own children (age eleven and 14) at the time my breast cancer was diagnosed. I was 19 at the time of my mother's death, still pretty mixed up and now having to deal with the shock and deep remorse I felt at not having realised how ill she was and having been away from home when she died.

In March 1968, aged 20, I married Roy, after knowing him for only six months. I had a miscarriage in May 1970, and then in August 1971 our son Matthew was born. I suffered from postnatal depression and was in and out of hospital, taking large amounts of anti-depressants and tranquillisers but unable to overcome my basic unhappiness, anxiety and anger. In May 1974 our daughter Louise was born, two months premature, weighing under 3 lb.

After her birth I noticed a definite pattern to my mood swings. The week or so preceding a period was a nightmare: I was depressed, angry and violent. I made several suicide attempts.

My husband's job took him abroad often, and during one trip I took an overdose and the children, aged six and three, ended up in care. I was taking large doses of Valium but feeling so anxious that going outside was almost impossible. I couldn't take or collect the children from school, do the shopping, or lead a normal life. I felt panicky if I was out and panicky if I was at home. Things seemed to have reached rock bottom. My faith was shaken; God seemed remote – how could he care about me when I couldn't even go to church? I was bitter and angry.

In retrospect it is very sad to think of life as it was. I had such a short time to enjoy my longed-for children, and I seemed to spend all my energy fighting the never relenting depression.

Gradually things improved, largely through my own efforts and the support of my husband. I began to venture out a little more, until one day in spring 1980 I spent a whole morning helping at the local playgroup. This proved to be a turning point. I took a job as a paid helper, then as my confidence increased became a supervisor. I had always loved children and found them easier to get on with than adults. Yet I still suffered from severe PMT and tried various treatments, expensive and painful, but none improved the situation much.

In January 1986, aged 38, when I discovered my breast cancer, I was working at playgroup several sessions a week. I was getting out and about, teaching in Sunday school and generally leading a more normal life. But I was still unhappy with myself and my inability to control my emotions. A shopping trip to Oxford was still an ordeal, due to panic attacks.

The planned operation on my breast went ahead – I amazed myself at how well I managed to get through it all, but I came home feeling pleased with myself because I had maintained my self-control. My faith in God was very real at this time; I felt able to trust him as never before and I was able to take courage from this and from the loving support of family and friends.

The surgeon who had operated on my breast had misled me into thinking that the cancer hadn't spread when, in fact, at my first appointment with the radiotherapy consultant I was told that the treatment would have to be very aggressive as the cancer involved my lymph nodes.

Chemotherapy was discussed and I went home 'to think about it'. How can one think about a course of action without relevant information? I needed to be fairly well informed before I could ask questions. I decided that chemotherapy seemed to offer a reasonable chance of destroying any cancer cells which might be lurking around, and began the recommended course. This turned out to be worse than I had anticipated; I found the nausea and vomiting very distressing and I had an allergic reaction to the anti-sickness drugs.

On the fourth course of treatment my husband and I were put in a side room, after the preliminary blood tests, and left waiting for an hour. The doctor then appeared with the prepared drugs and syringes. I began to cry, and he told me not to go ahead if I didn't feel like it – of course I didn't; who would? He told us that he would refrigerate the drugs and we could go away for an hour or so to decide what I wanted to do.

How could we decide what was best? All I knew was that I had reached the end of my endurance that day and I couldn't face the treatment. I was told, on my return, that if I didn't have the injections that day I might as well give up altogether. And that is what I did. But advice and counselling were nonexistent.

The radiotherapy went ahead as planned. I found it very difficult: lying trapped under huge machines, for four minutes at a time, was very claustrophobic – just the kind of situation which filled me with terror. But I developed a coping strategy, learning to relax by singing in my head, a favourite song being 'Be still and know that I am God'. I emerged from the radiotherapy badly burnt. It was impossible to wear any clothes for several days as they stuck to the burns.

I remember a Sunday school outing to Moreton-in-Marsh. As I didn't feel well enough to attempt the train journey with 50 or 60 children, Roy took me in the car and despite the painful burns and generally feeling unwell we had a lovely afternoon, surrounded by children and friends and sharing a picnic tea.

At this stage in the proceedings – July 1986 – I went to the Bristol Cancer Help Centre. I had read Kidman's *A Gentle Way With Cancer* and had watched the television programmes about the centre. Their approach was new and refreshing. No one even asked to see my breast; at the hospital that seemed to be their only area of interest. I was treated as a person; my dis-ease was considered.

The treatment I had received was excellent, and I was grateful that we were fortunate enough to live near such a good hospital, but I felt that I was treated as a carcinoma left breast and the rest of me was ignored. To me, it was a very personal thing: *my* cancer, a threat to my life, my courage, my faith in God, my entire existence.

I desperately needed to feel that I could still maintain some measure of control over my life and my destiny and come to terms with my illness and the way it affected me. My way of dealing with this was to meet it face on, and I needed to talk about it. My husband was very supportive, taking me to and from clinics, and looking after me through the side effects of the treatment. But his method of coping was the opposite to mine, being that if it wasn't thought or talked about it might actually go away.

The day we spent together at the BCHC was a revelation to me. I came away feeling positive about my illness and that I was able to take an active part in helping myself find wholeness. Apart from the cancer I was a very emotionally wounded and battered person.

I began to practise relaxation and meditation, and read the Simontons' book *Getting Well Again*. I found some of the recommendations about diet and supplements a bit way out, but we were largely vegetarian already, and I did cut out tea and coffee. So I took what I found helpful from Bristol.

Gradually, normal life resumed, and in September 1986 I was able to return to work at playgroup, eight months after I had left. But about six months after all the treatment ended the full impact of what had happened seemed to hit me. I had coped far better than I had believed possible at the time – now I went to pieces. In retrospect this was a very 'normal' reaction. I spent a couple of weeks in a psychiatric hospital, and it was at this time that I first met a psychiatrist who has become a kind and trusted friend over the years. He always sees me and Roy together, and for the first time I began to feel a lessening of the guilt and blame attached to always being labelled 'ill' – if not physically, then mentally.

The following summer we went as a family, and accompanied by my father, to Orkney, to visit my younger brother and his family, who have settled there. This trip presented me with a real challenge – train, boat and bus journeys – but I managed it, and the wonderful holiday was crowned with a sense of achievement.

My hospital check-ups had gradually lengthened to every six months and I was feeling very well and optimistic when in June 1988 I found a small lump in my right breast. The whole process began again. It was a tremendous blow to my confidence that after two and a half years the cancer had returned, and indeed to come to the realisation that all the time it had been silently lurking within my body.

I went ahead and had a lumpectomy, and returned to BCHC a week after the operation. Again I became determined to get the better of the disease, using whatever means I could: orthodox medicine, alternative medicine and Christian healing. I felt much more positive about myself as a person and my ability to cope with my illness.

The course of radiotherapy was not as intensive as the first time, as my lymph nodes were not involved. I employed much the same methods of coping, including visualisation learnt at Bristol and through the Simontons' book *Getting Well Again*. By October I was back at work, planning Christmas parties and nativity plays as usual.

The next year or so passed reasonably smoothly. Matthew left home in June 1989 to live and work in Oxford. One, for me, momentous occasion worth recording was that at the Christmas candlelight service on Christmas Eve 1989, I walked to the lectern in front of a packed church and read the lesson – Luke chapter 2: 'And there were in the same country shepherds abiding in the field'. The tremendous thing about it was that less than a year before I couldn't even sit in church without feelings of panic. The feeling of achievement was tremendous. Half the congregation were children, and from my work at playgroup I knew almost every child between the ages of twelve and three.

My work at playgroup continued and I became involved with setting up a new group of Rainbow Guides (five to seven year-olds;

pre-Brownies). Depression was still troublesome, but on the whole life was much more stable. I loved my work with children. Roy and I still saw Pepé the psychiatrist every couple of months or so.

In March 1990 I had what I assumed to be an ear infection, but although I went to the GP complaining of pain there was no infection. Then the pain seemed to be in my jaw and I saw my dentist, who told me it was nothing to worry about – as did my GP when I visited him again, even though by now the pain was unrelenting, like toothache and earache together, and my face was swollen.

By July there was no improvement and my doctor suggested ultrasound treatment. At the end of July I went to camp with the Guides, and I noticed that my right side felt stiff and painful sometimes, and by the end of the week my neck was also very stiff. But it seemed reasonable to suppose this could be the result of camping.

At a further visit to the doctor I was told to return in a week if my neck had not improved. Meanwhile the ultrasound treatment to my jaw continued, and when I mentioned my now ever-increasing catalogue of aches and pains to the physiotherapist, she wrote to my doctor. As a result of this, he carried out some blood tests which, he said, showed that I had arthritis. I was reassured by this, because I knew that breast cancer readily spreads to the bone, and I had been worried.

I voiced my concern to my GP and suggested a bone scan. There was a definite lump on my jaw, as well as pain in my ribs, neck and legs. I felt unwell and had lost $1^1/_2$ stones in weight. By this time it was August and we were due to visit our son in Canada. I was having difficulty walking, my neck was extremely painful, it was impossible to move my head a fraction of an inch without intense pain, and I spent some nights sitting propped up on the sofa, unable to sleep.

So I went again to my doctor, who arranged for me to see an arthritis specialist. The specialist immediately suggested a bone scan, and I was able to arrange this rapidly through a friend who is a radiographer. After an exhausting day of scans and Xrays I had to visit my GP yet again for the results. My suspicions were confirmed – I had metastases in my ribs, jaw and pelvis. Apparently nothing had shown up in my jaw in the scan, but I pointed out the swelling to the radiographer, who Xrayed it.

My neck was increasingly painful, and a further Xray revealed a critical situation: disease had almost destroyed the odontoid peg.

I was advised to cancel my holiday and have since learnt from one of the people who influenced this decision that she was torn between advising me to go and risk breaking my neck, or to stay and possibly never see my son again.

My husband and daughter went to Canada as planned and I stayed and had radiotherapy on my neck, jaw and pubic bone. Within six weeks I had changed from a busy, active person into a disabled one in a wheelchair, with my neck in a hard collar. But not only that, I had changed into a dying person.

I realised that this time the cancer was terminal, and this knowledge brought with it many conflicting emotions. One of the first things I felt was grief for my husband and children, and for the grandchildren I may never see. I was determined that if I had to die I would live life to the full until I died. I tried to find some purpose in my suffering. I prayed for healing.

I had to tell Matthew the state of affairs by telephone – a heartbreaking task. I wanted both children to know and understand what was happening and they have always been fully informed.

Roy and I spent a few days in the Yorkshire Dales. I wasn't very mobile, and encased in a hard collar, but managed a walk around Fountains Abbey, and the cream cakes from Betty's in Harrogate were a real treat.

Matthew came home in December and we had a lovely family Christmas, a poignant time – would it be our last? I had been forced to give up my job at playgroup and I found sitting in on the Christmas party very sad. I organised the costumes for the Sunday school nativity play as usual, but found it almost impossible to watch the children's performance. I felt so sad and unsure of my future.

The pain in my neck improved enormously, although I still wore a hard collar day and night. I was put on tamoxifen with no real effect, and had more palliative radiation to a rib which had fractured. Radiotherapy to my lower back and left hip became necessary in February, to help the pain.

In mid-March, Roy and I went to Florence and to Venice. Although walking was painful, I managed a full programme of sightseeing with my wheelchair. And at long last I had conquered my fear of flying. I wouldn't go so far as to say that I actually enjoyed it, but I did it, and the sight of the clouds beneath us illuminated by sunshine was incredible and unforgettable.

In April my left hip fractured, and one Monday afternoon I found myself in casualty. The consultant discussed his plan to pin the bone the following morning, but I insisted that I wanted to attend a wedding on the coming Thursday. The doctors, frankly, didn't seem too keen on letting me go home with a fractured neck of femur, but with encouragement from one of the nurses to stick up for what I wanted, I arranged to be readmitted on the Friday, the day after the wedding.

I should explain that this was no ordinary wedding. My friend was marrying for the second time and Roy and I had been asked to be witnesses – no one else knew about it. We had a very special day, and I duly presented myself at the hospital on the Friday.

The surgeon had decided that my hip was too badly diseased to pin, and so I underwent a hip replacement under an epidural as my neck and jaw were still unstable. My recovery was quick, and on the whole the week's stay in hospital was uneventful.

One incident does, however, stand out. I suffered from headaches as a result of the epidural, and about three days after the operation a blood patch was done. Some blood was drawn, via a cannula, and injected into my spine, the idea being that the blood would clot and seal the small hole where fluid was leaking. This went well, and the cannula was left in place as it had been discovered that I needed a blood transfusion.

A young woman doctor came with the blood, but it would not flow through the cannula in my right arm. So she proceeded to make two attempts on my left arm, with complete and total disregard for me. I was, by this time, near to the end of my endurance. One kind word, or even an acknowledgement that attached to that arm was a person, would have made so much difference to me.

Instead I sat on the bed with tears silently streaming down my face, more from lack of simple caring than pain. A word of encouragement, a touch or a smile, can make so much difference to the situation. Patients are people, and what is more we are frequently frightened and feeling extremely vulnerable.

While having radiation treatment planned to my hip, I was lying on a table. Although the consultant surgeon came to look at the Xrays, he didn't even look my way, let alone acknowledge my presence. I wish I had had the courage to sit up and say, 'Good morning. By the way, attached to this hip is a living, rather insecure person.' Just a couple of words would have made so much difference.

Medical students should be taught much more about patients as people. Before my second breast operation I was asked if I minded students coming in with the consultant. I readily agreed, and all went well. But after the physical examination and chat the consultant and ten students went just outside the door and proceeded to discuss my case within my hearing and that of my two room-mates, who had no idea why I was there until then.

Dignity is very important, too. I had an eight-minute radiotherapy treatment to my pubic bone, and was told by the radiographers not to take my underwear off, just to slip it down. But did they not consider what it felt like to be lying on the treatment table for eight minutes with my knickers round my knees? I felt thoroughly miserable and humiliated: a blanket over my underwear and knees would have meant so much.

Summer 1991 was spent doing all sorts of things which I had thought I would never again be able to manage. We spent two weekends at a friend's caravan in Wales and only six weeks after the hip replacement I climbed up and down to Welsh beaches and walked on the sand. We also spent two weekends in Norfolk, and on one occasion I walked about 2 miles over tidal marshes to an island and returned, after a picnic lunch, in a small ferry. I climbed in at one end, and walked down a gangplank at the other!

A particular joy has been my ability to walk again in Wychwood forest, a place which I love and I had thought would not be accessible again. Being able to go on these walks was taken for granted a couple of years ago: this summer they meant so much more because I had thought I would never do them again. My life has been enriched in so many ways through the experience of cancer.

It is now November 1991. Having cancer has been a very educational process for me, and I have met so much love and help along the way. I still sometimes think, why me? The age-old question of why we have to suffer has not been fully answered, but I do know now that suffering can be used to bring about a greater trust and confidence in God, and also in oneself. I now feel very secure in the knowledge that God is very close to me in my pain. As this quote from *Healing Experiences* by Howard Booth[1] says:

> Suffering should not be embraced, nor should it be passively accepted. Often it is a challenge to us to summon up all our own

resources and seek all the help we can from others so that our suffering can be fought, resisted and overcome. If we just deny it or sit down under it we may fail to discover what our suffering is saying to us.

So why choose me to endure this? I'm not tough enough, I haven't the strength and courage. In fact, I'm an extremely bad candidate with my long history of anxiety and depression. I am not special; I am just an ordinary person having to deal with cancer. But if I can do it, then so can anyone.

Why was I selected to take on this task? I believe that it was to lead me to wholeness and healing and that I am discovering these gifts through my suffering. I have grown enormously, emotionally and spiritually. I needed to come to terms with my illness, and in doing that I am being freed to find healing in and through it.

I have learnt to trust God, and other people, and to ask for help. I have found a stronger faith, and I am certain that wherever I am, in pain, terror, depression, God is always there beside me. My courage has increased enormously with this knowledge.

In a strange way having cancer has given me a purpose in life which was lacking before. It is certainly a challenge – just to get up each day and live with it, but much more to try to bring something positive out of the experience. With my increasing confidence in God, my old angers and bitterness have largely vanished. I have found so much love and support from family, friends, doctors and nurses, and I have become much more secure and able to accept love and help without the old fear of rejection. And, I think, more able to give something back to other people.

Healing isn't necessarily physical healing, but wholeness, and a tremendous amount of healing has taken place in me. I have discovered various allies along the way – relaxation, meditation, yoga, massage, aromatherapy.

I am thankful for the people I have met – friends who have encouraged me enormously and supported me with cards, letters, phone calls, prayers, love and their confidence in me. For the doctors I have met, and the nurses who have looked after me, and for the nurses and volunteers at Sir Michael Sobell House, our local hospice. For fellow patients, for their friendship, courage and humour. For a chance meeting with a priest in Walsingham, and the relationship which has developed, and for the friendship of Pepé. And for the concern of so many people, too numerous to mention.

There is still an enormous stigma attached to cancer, but I think that it is most important to let people know that the disease is not an immediate death sentence. I am alive and reasonably well, I lead a very full life. I am a survivor and so are thousands of others. We should let people know.

Our illness may be terminal – life is terminal! A patient support group has been set up at Sir Michael Sobell House and this is an encouraging development. We have been asked to video a group session for teaching purposes. I was asked a few weeks ago if I would allow a medical student to interview me about my feelings. So things are changing.

I am, at the moment, deciding whether to undergo some palliative radiotherapy to my pelvis. This time I feel that I am firmly in control. I have learnt to become more assertive and to fit my treatment into my life rather than having to fit my life around my treatment.

Undergoing a bone scan recently I asked if I could use my walkman. The technician said, 'No one ever asked before.' So I was able to listen to Pavarotti and recall, while having my scan, a wet but very memorable day spent in Hyde Park. What a difference from lying alone and afraid looking at the ceiling!

As for the future – who knows – there is so much to look forward to. Maybe another trip to Italy in the spring? A great joy, being godmother to my friend's baby daughter in January, and a party in July to celebrate several special family birthdays.

I only visited Bristol Cancer Help Centre twice, and I was one of the first women who in July 1986 took part in the ICR survey of women with breast cancer. I have returned for a day of sharing with other such women. I always feel a sense of caring and peace when I go through the front door. Although I haven't been an avid follower of their philosophy, a lot of their suggestions have helped me in the journey I am undertaking, and I feel a lasting gratitude to them for helping me to see my disease and my life differently.

Sometimes I still feel angry. I often feel vulnerable, but I rarely feel alone. People's kindness and generosity continue to help me. Throughout it all I have retained a sense of humour. I am a different person, I have changed, and it seems sad that the change has had to come about with the onset of a life-threatening illness, but I am thankful that the change has taken place.

I have wonderful friends. I couldn't manage without their support and their confidence in my ability to continue to be me; somewhat scarred by my experiences but nevertheless a whole person. I like to be treated as I always was, but for people not to ignore what is happening to me, because cancer has become a part of my life whether I like it or not.

I end with a quote from *The Road Less Travelled* by M. Scott Peck:[2]

People handle their fear of change in different ways, but the fear is inescapable if they are in fact to change. Courage is not the absence of fear; it is the making of action in spite of fear, and moving out against the resistance engendered by fear into the unknown and into the future. On some level spiritual growth and therefore love always requires courage and involves risk … Move out or grow in any dimension and pain as well as joy will be your reward. A full life will be full of pain. But the only alternative is not to live fully or not to live at all.

Notes and References

1   Booth, H. *Healing Experiences* 1985; London: Bible Reading Fellowship, p. 28.
2   Scott Peck, M., *The Road Less Travelled* 1985; London: Century Hutchinson, pp. 131–3.

8 Fighting Spirit

June Shaw

June was 53 when her cancer was diagnosed in 1977, and she only went to Bristol when it recurred. She died in the autumn of 1994, aged 70, and her story is told by her second husband Fred, a retired general practitioner.

June was born in Edinburgh on 4 June 1924, and at an early age was given to an uncle and aunt to bring up. June was never really sure why, but presumed it was for financial reasons.

June's uncle and aunt lived in the country, her uncle being a gamekeeper. They were very strict with June, almost to the point of cruelty. Poor little June had to make do with everything either secondhand or homemade. At one time she asked her uncle if she could have two swords for her Scottish dancing class: he gave her two lengths of steel rod. I can well imagine her embarrassment in front of her schoolfriends. In spite of this and many other embarrassing moments, June grew up to be a most normal, level-headed person, and in no way embittered.

She went to the local school, which meant a 3-mile walk each way, summer and winter. June was a bright child and eventually passed on to the senior school. On leaving school she joined the bank, where she worked until she was old enough to volunteer for the Wrens in 1943. Because of her bank training she was put in the paymaster's department, much to her annoyance, as she wanted above all to be a motorcycle despatch rider. Part of her work was going on board ships to pay the crew. On one of these trips she met Chief Petty Officer Reg Rawle, fell in love and got married in 1946.

June was eventually demobbed, but Reg was still in the Navy and his ship, a mine-sweeper, was transferred to Cork. June followed and found digs in the city of Cork. She was always full of praise for the kindness, generosity and help she received from the local people.

Finally Reg's ship was moved elsewhere and June came to live in Bideford, a town in north Devon, with Reg's parents, in early 1947. Later that same year Reg was demobbed and joined June.

He got a job as manager of a mill 4 or 5 miles outside the town; a cottage went with the job, and June and Reg promptly moved in. They were happy to be together in their own little place. It was, however, an old cottage, and did not have modern facilities: no lights, only oil lamps; no water, only an outside tap; no indoor toilet. Bathing meant heating water and pouring it into a bath in front of the kitchen fire. June was wonderful. She took everything in her stride, never complaining, but counting her blessings instead.

In May 1947 I came to Bideford to join a group practice of doctors. I was not in Bideford very long before I met June, who came to see me for some not very serious complaint, and from then on, whenever she needed advice or treatment she came to see me.

In 1949 her first baby arrived in the early hours of the morning. It was a long labour, and when number one son arrived he was a bit shocked, and I quickly passed him over to the midwife while I waited for the afterbirth. When all was over and June and baby were washed and settled down, I asked her if she would like me, on my way home, to call and tell her family the good news. Before I left to spread the good tidings I asked the midwife if it was a boy or a girl. 'A girl' was the reply, so off I went to tell the family.

Reg had a large number of relatives in Cornwall, and June also had relations in Scotland. As soon as the post office opened, telegrams were flying off to all parts of the United Kingdom. Later that morning the mistake was discovered and a second batch of telegrams was soon putting things to rights. Reg never allowed me to forget my *faux pas*, but good-naturedly continued to remain a loyal patient.

Two years later number two son arrived without any bizarre happenings. Not long afterwards June, Reg and their two young sons moved into the Mill House proper. This was absolute heaven. They now had electricity, indoor sanitation and a bathroom – no more bathing in front of the kitchen fire. Apart from being a wife and mother and organising and running a home, June became the clerk to the mill office. Nothing was too much trouble for her, and she was certainly not afraid of hard work. As time moved on and the two young sons grew up, June took on yet another job: she became a hospital car driver, ferrying patients to and from hospital. During these years I saw very little of the family; I think they were all too busy to be sick.

Number one son got married and emigrated to Australia. Number two son also married, but his work was in the immediate neighbourhood. June and Reg were on various village committees and ran whist drives, bingo and skittles and took a very lively interest in the village fête. June even embroidered an altar cushion for the village church.

One day in 1977 June came into my surgery and said: 'Doc, I think I have a lump in my breast.' When I examined her there was absolutely no doubt that she had a lump, and it was fixed both to the skin and the underlying tissues. I got her an urgent appointment to see a surgeon, who promptly took her into hospital, removed the lump and followed this with a course of chemotherapy. June was frequently checked up and had further courses of the dreaded chemotherapy.

In 1981 my own wife became an invalid and I found myself in a cleft stick, tied to looking after both my wife and my patients, and I felt that I was not being fair to either so I opted for early retirement. My wife died on 25 March 1983.

Now alone after two years of retirement, I began to wonder what was the purpose of life any more. My love, my constant companion, my strong right arm and adviser was gone. I felt inadequate, miserable and full of self-pity. Gradually it dawned on me that I was not the only one who had been through a similar experience, and that life must go on. It used to annoy me when people would say 'Time is a great healer'. To me that is a trite expression that rolls easily off the tongue: I do not agree with it.

One day while out shopping I happened to bump into June. I asked her how she was and she said: 'I'm fine by day but the nights are awful.' Not long after going to bed the pain would start in her right shoulder, and the only relief she could get was to go downstairs and sit with her back pressed against the Rayburn stove for warmth. I asked her what her new doctor was doing for this. Typical of June, not wanting to be a nuisance, she had not reported it to her GP. I made her promise then and there to go and see her doctor as soon as possible.

Repeated examinations and Xrays showed nothing abnormal, but in spite of this the pain persisted and eventually a scan showed metastases in the humerus and in some of the ribs, and her treatment was changed. It was felt that her previous treatment was no longer being effective. Slowly but surely the pain began to ease off.

For ten or more years June had become very interested in silver, especially antique silver, and she became quite an expert on the subject. She had a stall at the local weekly antique market, where she quickly became a popular member with all the other stallholders.

As June's ups and downs became more frequent she heard of the Bristol Cancer Help Centre, but could not afford to go. Her fellow stallholders helped to raise the necessary cash, and June went to Bristol.

In her group in Bristol there were eight in all, coming from all parts of the country, and one from Dublin. At the end of the week June found she was refreshed, encouraged, with a new zest for living and a renewed fighting spirit. She returned home with a list of the others in her group – names and addresses in no particular order. Over the years the friends on June's list died in the exact order that they appeared, June herself being the last to go. Was this just an incredible coincidence?

June carried on in her own inimitable style for the next few years, attending Bristol once a year as a day visitor. Then suddenly in 1988 Reg was struck down with a heart attack, and immediately admitted to hospital. There June was told that the first 48 hours were critical. Reg responded rapidly to treatment and was told that if his condition continued to improve he would probably be allowed home in three or four days. However, on the seventh day Reg had a sudden cardiac arrest, to which he succumbed.

I had got into the habit of dropping in to have a chat with Leno, Reg and June's nephew, who owned a restaurant, on a Saturday morning before opening time. This particular morning I breezed in full of the joys of spring only to be met with the very sad news of Reg's death. The family were in the house at the time, so I told Leno that I would disappear and not intrude on their grief. However, the family suddenly appeared and June, on seeing me, threw her arms round my neck and burst into floods of tears. I told June's younger son Ian that if there was anything I could do, just to let me know.

Later that evening Ian rang me to ask if I could drop in the next day and have a chat with June. This I did. There were one or two questions that June wanted answered, and I was able to put her mind at rest. I stayed with her for perhaps an hour and then I felt she had had enough, and left June and Ian to their own thoughts.

I attended the funeral later in the week; the church was crowded and I did not get a chance to speak to any of the family.

About three months later June invited me out to tea at the mill. I was amazed at how well she was coping with life. There was only one thing worrying me: she was surviving on cups of tea and bread and butter; she was not cooking for herself, and she was a superb cook. As I was leaving I asked her if she would come out and have lunch with me one day. After that we started seeing each other quite regularly, and phoning each other in between times.

Some time later I asked June: 'When a respectable length of time has passed, would you do me the honour of becoming my wife?' To my absolute delight she said: 'Yes.'

June's elder son Michael, who had emigrated to Australia 20 years earlier, invited June and her cousin Anna, who lived in Scotland, to come out for a holiday and a change of scene. Ian and I saw them off. To me it was a sad parting, but I knew that they were going to have a wonderful time, which indeed they did. When you have just got engaged, six weeks apart is an awfully long time, but eventually June and Anna came home.

While they were both in Australia, I arranged a little trip for June and myself, providing June was fit enough. Happily she was very fit, so I told her that I had booked us a trip on the Orient Express to Salzburg, where we would spend a few days. We would then travel by coach through the Austrian Lake District to Linz, where we would board Concorde and fly back to Heathrow. An unforgettable trip, and that was a very definite plus for a couple, one with cancer and the other over 70 years of age.

We went to Normandy for the forty-fifth Anniversary of D-Day: plus number two. We went up to Scotland and took a log cabin for three weeks. We were there for the lambing season. The lambs were the loveliest either of us had ever seen: jet black faces, brilliant white coats and two little black patches on their knees, just as though they had been kneeling in the mud. Another plus.

June, being Scottish, was very proud of her homeland, and rightly so. Three weeks in the good clear air of the Highlands, with the tranquillity and magnificence of the scenery, did her a power of good.

I see I have omitted to mention the fact that June and I had a very quiet wedding in the local registry office on 1 December 1990, with only Ian, my daughter Lesley and my grandson Merlin being present, which was the way we both wanted it.

June was seeing the consultant about every three months, and if she complained of anything different he immediately had it thoroughly investigated. He could not have been kinder, more attentive or reassuring, and never took anything June said lightly. June had two older sisters, both widows, one living in Yorkshire and the other in Stirling. Sister Babs from Stirling died in March 1993 from abdominal cancer. June and I drove up for the funeral. The burial took place in a most picturesque cemetery at the foot of a hill, 4 or 5 miles out in the country. At night the rabbits would come down and eat the flower heads of the carnations, just leaving the bare stalks.

During this time June appeared to be remarkably well, but then she very seldom complained, being much more concerned about other people's health. I had a very dear old friend who was in her ninetieth year, Mrs Allen, and I said to her one day (this was before June and I were married) that I would like to introduce her to the bravest person that I had ever known, and I went on to describe June to her.

A few days later Mrs Allen was at a Conservative ladies' luncheon, and it so happened that June had also been invited. I told Mrs Allen, and she made a special point of introducing herself to June. After that they became firm friends. Sadly, Mrs Allen died in 1992 at the age of 91, but with a mind as clear and sharp as a 20-year-old. She was out for her daily walk, and dropped dead in the street. We missed her very much.

In September 1993 we decided that we would like to go to Normandy in June 1994 for the fiftieth anniversary of D-Day. We made this decision although it was still eight to nine months away, and we joined an Airborne Forces organised trip.

Late in November June suddenly became very ill with severe abdominal pain. She was rushed into hospital where everyone, myself included, thought that this was the end. But none of us allowed for June's courage, fighting spirit and will to live. For three weeks she was at death's door, and then she just decided that enough was enough and asked to be allowed home. By this time the pain had largely subsided, though she was still taking fairly strong painkillers. June came home after another week in hospital. She was pale, very weak, and had lost an awful lot of weight. The same day she came home her elder son and his wife arrived from Australia. This did June no end of good.

Not long afterwards it was Christmas Day and June was happy to have her two sons with her on such a joyous occasion. She was gradually regaining her strength and putting on some weight. I never ceased to marvel at her powers of recovery and will to live.

Michael and his wife from 'down under' had to return home at the end of January 1994, and June was well enough by then to go 40-odd miles to see them off. It was a sad parting, as I feel both of them knew that it was for the last time. Again June was wonderful.

As the weeks went by June's health gradually improved, though her walking was limited. By now it was getting near our trip to Normandy, and I told June that I was going to cancel it. June got quite indignant and refused to let me. On 3 June we left Bideford and travelled up to London. The next day, June's birthday, we crossed the Channel to France and stayed in the pretty little town of Honfleur. In the morning we went by coach to Ranville, one of the sites of the D-Day airborne landings, and witnessed many commemorative services. It was tiring for June, but luckily we had a folding chair, and she was able to sit and get her breath back as necessary. In the evening we returned to Honfleur, had an early dinner and retired to bed, tired but happy.

The next day, D-Day, it was back to Ranville to watch a mass parachute drop. We were to have taken part in a march-past before Prince Charles. Unfortunately we got stuck in traffic, which was horrendous, and never got to our starting point. I was told afterwards that the Prince waited half an hour to give us a chance to get there, but owing to a very busy schedule he could not wait any longer. Later, however, we attended a service at the British Airborne Cemetery at which Her Royal Highness the Princess Margaret honoured us with her presence.

Next morning, 7 June, we travelled back home. At that time I did not anticipate that four months to the day June would be taken from us. She had been absolutely marvellous and, with hindsight, I feel had pushed herself to the hilt so that I could be present in Normandy. I know she enjoyed it, especially as she herself had done her bit in the Wrens; she was relaxed, happy and, I know, proud to be there.

At home life returned to the usual household duties and our mutual interest in doing jigsaw puzzles together. June had some delightful little expressions all of her own. She would say to me, not being able to find the next piece: 'I have come to a stuck', which would mean that we just changed places and carried on. We spent many a very happy hour together, just the two of us, doing simple things.

Gradually during August 1994 June noticed that she was becoming increasingly breathless and, on seeking medical advice, she was given oxygen. We kept a cylinder of oxygen in the lounge, and another in the bedroom. This gave June relief, but gradually I noticed that she was relying on it more and more. The consultant came to the house to see her and decided he wanted to take her into hospital for investigation. His hospital was 45 miles away. An admission was duly arranged, and I took June in on Wednesday 28 September. She had two days of investigations and was allowed home for the weekend, for readmission on Monday 3 October.

I used to visit her every day. Each day she was weaker, and on Thursday 6 October she had been sleeping off and on while I was there. She suddenly said to me: 'You had better go home now as I want to go to sleep.' At that time I did not realise that those were to be the last words she would ever say to me.

We only had three years and ten months of married life together, but they were so happy, and although I miss my June so very much it would only be pure selfishness on my part to wish her back to a life of suffering.

On 12 October June was buried with Reg, as we had agreed. When my turn comes I shall be buried with my first wife, Joan. Still we shall, I know, all meet again in a place where there is no more suffering. I am still grief-stricken enough to hope it won't be too far away.

June won every battle but the last one.

Fred Shaw ended his story with the words: 'God bless you, darling. FRED.' June lived for 17 years from her first diagnosis of cancer to her death. Sadly, Dr Shaw himself only lived for another eight months after June's death, and died of cancer on 20 June 1995. This was exactly a year after his memorable visit to Normandy with June.

9 One of Life's Mysteries

Joanna Treseder

Joanna wrote her own account of her cancer experience soon after the *Lancet* report was published in 1990. She was only 34 when she first found a lump in her breast, in 1980. In 1987 the lump was removed; she died in 1991. Her story is introduced by her second husband, Les.

Introduction by Joanna's husband, Les Tocknell

There is one certainty about cancer: it frightens the life out of you. There are many factors which may be taken into account to explain the disease – pollution, food additives, lifestyle, stress, genetic disposition, personality, hormones, diet, radiation and more – but when you sit there absorbing the diagnosis delivered by your doctor, however humanly this is done, it is the fear that grips you, drags you down, knots you up and ultimately will destroy you, if you let it.

I am not writing as a cancer patient. I can tell you now, I hope I never will write from that perspective. I fear every lump, bump, ache or pain I feel in case it is cancer. I even fear weight loss when I know I am overweight and am trying to trim down.

No, I was that watcher and waiter, the 'carer' (although I had little of that to do): the partner, the husband ('hubby' as you become to the staff on the hospital ward). There were times when I believed my fear was greater than Joanna's, although I cannot now imagine that that can have been so. To me, the earth-bound materialist, the unimaginable is not to be here. To Joanna, it was all a spiritual journey with the knowledge, reinforced by Kübler-Ross's work, that there would be light at the end of the tunnel. For me, I had only life, then death. I do not think this is helpful. I certainly came to understand the *need* to believe.

I went through agonies after Joanna died, hoping for a sign, a clue, that she was close by, on the 'other side'. Spiritual enlightenment does not come that easily, as Joanna's story, most of it told in her own words, will show. What I did learn is that if there is something you want to do, and there is nothing stopping you other than your own reticence, inertia, inhibition – then do it! When you know you are dying and weakness disables you, it is too late.

Joanna's story is about learning that lesson early enough. She did, but at a cost. The cost was to deny herself conventional treatment in the form of chemotherapy because she knew it would prevent her from *living* her life, however short it was to be. It would have prevented her from being *herself*. She believed that the principles of the programme devised by the Bristol Cancer Help Centre would enable her to live the rest of her life in the way she wanted to. That was why I believe the *Lancet* report was a major blow to her. She died a year after it was published. I could blame that research, but I could never prove the link. It does make me angry, though. She may have died earlier because she chose not to have chemotherapy, but she died better. Can you understand that? For her a long, empty life was *not* preferable to a short, full one.

She was not naïve. She had a medical training as a nurse. She knew the score. I was more naïve and I think she kept me so because she recognised my fear. It seems that the only way to overcome that fear is to believe in what you are doing. And that is what the researchers did not understand. I am convinced that if there were a similar report condemning the efficacy of radiotherapy or chemotherapy there would be a large number of early deaths among current and ex-patients of those treatments.

Please do not read this and think: 'What a wonderful person, a saint to bear her cross this way. I could never emulate her.' This was a journey, and like many journeys it was cut short, and like many journeys there were wrong turns and blind alleys, because, however good the map, we always have to rely on the skill of the navigator. In spiritual matters, the maps are notoriously unreliable anyway.

Joanna's path threaded its way between ferocity and despair. The ferocity, frightening if directed towards you, was what enabled her to face her illness. It was her ferocity that inspired her to ride an adult tricycle along the Camel trail in Cornwall with her arm in a sling. It needed pinning after radiotherapy treatment left the bone almost severed. It was her ferocious appetite for life which led her to surf, learn to helm a dinghy, go to African dance lessons, take on a demanding job, all in her last year. Her GP tasted that ferocity when on her last night she lectured him on the difference between 'giving up' and 'letting go', because she no longer wished to be kept alive with chemotherapy.

And the despair ... principally, the despair in the knowledge that she would never hold her own baby. Joanna died on 30 November 1991.

Joanna's story in her own words

The background

The story starts when I first developed a lump in my breast in 1980, aged 34 years. At the time I was already having problems with conception and had started having investigations for infertility. I was only at the beginning of what has proved to be an extremely painful and difficult time of my life, and I feel sure that this is inextricably linked to my developing cancer. The fact that I had cancer of my right breast is significant to me too. When I thought that I would have a child, I always imagined breastfeeding it. In Eastern philosophy the right side is looked on as the giving, active side; the left as the receptive, passive side. When a mother breastfeeds her child, she is 'giving' to it in the most fundamental way that she can.

Initially I saw two local consultants about my infertility, one of whom carried out some investigations (a D and C and tubal insufflation). The other prescribed a hysterectomy if I got any worse (for some years I had had crippling periods which often forced me to stay in bed for at least a day). Neither of them were successful in discovering what or just how much had gone wrong with my reproductive system. (My work lies, now, in letting go of all the difficulties and pain of these past years.) Eventually, after strenuous requests to my then GP, I was referred to Mr S. He carried out a laparoscopy, saw at once that my tubes and uterus were extensively damaged, and referred me to Professor E. at the Withington Hospital in Manchester. One of his first comments to me was, 'I wish you'd got to me sooner.' It was then the late summer of 1984.

However, he agreed to operate on me, and was successful in unblocking one of my fallopian tubes, re-siting my ovaries and repairing my uterus. Extensive damage had been caused by a low-grade infection that had probably been present for some years. Professor E. was the first doctor who was prepared to admit that the infection had very probably been caused by a copper IUD, of which I had had several over about four to five years. It is now, of course, thought by many doctors that women who have not had and may want children should not be fitted with IUDs. Ever since having that surgery, my periods have been painless and straightforward, which has been an inestimable relief and great joy to me.

About two years before I had the surgery my then partner and I applied to the local authority for adoption. We were initially turned down and appealed against this decision, the grounds of which were not given, and after a protracted application time we were eventually accepted. By this time, however, the stresses and strains of all that had been happening had begun to affect our relationship, and by the time I was admitted to the Withington, we had separated.

When my present husband and I began living together, we thought it would be as well for him to have a sperm count – the results of which showed that his count was low. So then began another series of visits to the Withington for sperm tests, postcoital tests and blood tests to check my ovulation, and to another hospital for two hysterosalpingograms for me, which showed one fallopian tube open, the other possibly so.

In March 1987 my present partner and I married, and not long afterwards, decided to apply once again to the local authority for adoption. (In May, after a long series of strokes, my father died.) This time the approach was very different, and our application was going well when I was admitted to hospital again to have a lump in my breast removed. When we knew that the lump had been cancerous we decided to have our adoption application put 'on the shelf' until we knew whether I would have to have any further treatment or not. When we reopened our application, we heard after several weeks that the Ministry of Health was of the opinion that my having had a cancerous breast lump meant that I should not be considered for adoption.

This somewhat lengthy account may not appear to be actually about 'my experience of cancer', but I feel that it is directly related. Looking back now, I realise that I was under constant stress of different sorts for five to six years. Both I and my then partner were in great need of counselling help and support. Penny Brohn, in her book *The Bristol Programme*, lists three characteristics, some or all of which often seem to be true of cancer patients. They are people who (1) have difficulty expressing negative emotions; (2) often enjoy helping others, and may have a tendency towards 'do-gooding'; (3) have a low self-image, low self-esteem. She also mentions a theory that the Swiss psychiatrist Carl Jung had about cancer, that in some people it is the negative manifestation of creative energy that for some reason has been blocked and unable to find an expressive outlet.

When I read that, it made complete sense to me: more than that, I felt it was speaking directly to me, that it offered me some understanding of why I had developed cancer. Looking at the other three points, the first is certainly true of me – I come from a family where so-called 'negative' emotions were rarely expressed, with the result that I too have great difficulty in expressing them. As to the second point, I don't see myself as a 'do-gooder' but I have been in various 'helping professions' for most of my life. I didn't think the third point described me either, until a friend pointed out that during the period of my separation and divorce my self-esteem was very low.

Joanna's story breaks off here, but the following extract is taken from a letter she wrote to the Debra Stappard Trust, who supported her during the time she followed the Gerson therapy: a very rigorous nutritional programme.

Letter to the Debra Stappard Trust, 1990

I want to thank you all – a tremendously big thank you – for supporting me in the way that you are doing. Without your help I wouldn't have been able to carry on doing the Gerson and eating in the way that I feel I need to – i.e. organically. It is so expensive. Fortunately, however, we've got a wonderful local person who grows organic fruit and veg, and I buy as much as I can directly from her. I still spend about £40 a week on other basics, which she cannot provide, from an organic wholesaler 40 miles away. Medicines are the other big expenditure, although I have been able to reduce some of these now.

My breast cancer was first diagnosed almost exactly three years ago. Not only was there the shock of the diagnosis, but Les, my husband, and I were in the process of applying for adoption and my diagnosis, of course, brought that to an abrupt halt.

I had a lumpectomy and, as I felt physically quite fit soon after, I continued my work as a counsellor/therapist. I developed another lump, however, early the following year – and again had a lumpectomy. Soon after my diagnosis I visited the Bristol

Cancer Help Centre for a day, which I found very helpful. That visit introduced me to healing and I found a wonderful healer, Julia, in the Lake District, where we then lived, who was enormously supportive. I had to make an 80-mile round trip to visit her, however, and much of the other support I would have liked – a counsellor/therapist for myself, for example – was not available. I changed my diet radically but found it almost impossible to obtain organic food. Things have progressed tremendously on many fronts in the last three years!

My counselling training is in an approach called 'psychosynthesis', which I find wonderfully rich and nourishing. Indeed, without my training, and the support I have received from friends and therapists within psychosynthesis, I don't believe that I would have been able to confront and work with my cancer in the way that I have done. One of the key approaches of psychosynthesis is that it sees us all in a spiritual as well as a very human dimension. To put it another way, we all have vast reservoirs of untapped and unfulfilled potential – as well as the many problems with which our lives and our personalities confront us.

I believe that personal tragedy and life-threatening diseases often (although not always) befall us when we have become blocked and/or when we have lost our direction in life. The desperate plights in which we find ourselves can, often, act as a catalyst towards enormous breakthrough and change. I believe that that has certainly been true of myself.

In June of the year when I had had a second breast lump removed, I developed a third lump – as I was on my way to an international psychosynthesis conference in Italy. I went to the conference and, on my return home, discovered that my consultant was on holiday. Another lovely consultant stepped in and actually came and visited me at home. He agreed to do a third lumpectomy but said that, as my breasts are very small, any further lumpectomies wouldn't be possible and a mastectomy would be, in his view, the only option.

After that surgery I travelled to Devon to have a course of radiotherapy, as the radiotherapy I was offered in the North sounded very disfiguring and unnecessarily strong in side effects. I not only had no side effects in Devon but was able to swim every day – which I always find very, very therapeutic. By the time I got to Devon I had a post-operative enlarged lymph node under my arm, which I hadn't noticed and which was another great shock. However, the radiotherapy was successful in dealing with that.

Every day I lay down, relaxed to a tape and did creative visualisation. I also spent a lot of time holding and touching my breast, and asked Les to do so too. Touch, by yourself and others, seems a vital part of healing to me. I am about to go on a weekend course in Radiance technique – which a friend of mine practises and which is a way of channelling universal energy into ourselves using the Chakra centres of Eastern philosophy. My friend gave me regular Radiance technique sessions while I was staying with her in Devon and receiving my radiotherapy.

All was well, then, for a while. I decided I must give up work and devote more time and energy to myself and healing. Then I started getting fluid collections on my breast. The first couple of times, tests showed that the fluid contained no abnormal cells, but the third time it did. When the results came through I was in London on a selection course to become a tutor for the Family Planning Association. By that time I had read Beata Bishop's book *A Time to Heal*, and decided that I would do the Gerson if my cancer recurred. So I was all set – as soon as my old friend in Cornwall had said he would finance me. I decided, however, that I couldn't possibly do the therapy in the remote part of the Lakes in which we lived and that I would have to move to London. An old friend offered me the use of a bedsit and a small kitchen in her house – and off I went.

Les, meanwhile, had decided that visiting me in London from the Lake District would be impossible, so he started looking for jobs in the South. A job came up in Gloucestershire, as manager of a day centre for adults with mental handicaps, which was his job in the Lakes – he applied and got the job. So before I left for London we put our house on the market, sold it (after the usual traumas), househunted and found a small terrace house in the Forest of Dean. After I had gone to London, however, that house purchase fell through, sending us once again into chaos and confusion – Les was desperate. Again, we were wonderfully lucky and were able to buy the house next door.

I often feel that the stress and strain on the partner or family of someone with cancer is at least as great, if not greater, than on the person herself (or himself), and I do feel that that has been true of Les. He has been the most wonderful source of support: with him I have been able to shout, scream, laugh and cry fountains. One of the things I would like to see is far greater support for people close to those with cancer.

Although the Gerson is incredibly hard work, I felt that I did very well on it, until in about March this year I developed a secondary in the upper bone of my left arm. A bone scan showed other small spots in some ribs and in my skull. I had another course of radiotherapy – to my arm – and was put on Provera (a hormone drug) by my consultant. All seemed to be well until my arm, six weeks or so on, began to feel very painful again. An Xray showed that the radiotherapy, in disintegrating my tumour, had left practically no bone intact, and by the time I got to the hospital my arm was hanging by a thread! I was admitted from out-patients as an emergency to have my arm pinned.

Since then it has repaired well, and a further bone scan showed that the spots in my ribs and skull had healed. I was unable to drive for some time, but one of my two terrific helpers agreed to taxi me in return for the use of my car when I didn't need it.

A wonderful week's holiday in Tenby in the summer seemed to 'put me back into my body'. I swam, surfed, sailed and, contrary to all Gerson rules, sunbathed! Soon after that I started driving again.

Since September I have had the use of a friend's flat in Bristol, and I come here for three to four days a week. There are many things here that I feel I very much need. I go to several evening classes – writing, Tai Chi and African dance (the latter is one of the best discoveries I've ever made). There is also an ozone swimming pool here (chlorine is an absolute 'no' when on the Gerson and I find it disagrees with me) and I swim every week. I also love being where there's lots of activity after having been housebound for so long. I've just started exploring doing some voluntary work too.

I'm now doing a very modified Gerson. I usually make one huge carrot and apple juice first thing (about $1\frac{1}{2}$ pints), a large green juice some time in the morning and another carrot and apple late afternoon. I've widened my diet, but still eat very strictly (except for occasional lapses/treats which now feel very therapeutic). My body now tells me what it wants or doesn't want, likes or dislikes, and I've learnt to listen to it.

The enclosed photo was taken about ten days after the surgery to my arm when Les and I had a holiday booked in Cornwall (which is where I come from). The tricycle ride was initially terrifying, but the psychological effect of completing a 10-mile ride on a beautiful cycle track running alongside an estuary was another important milestone for me.

At the same period, Joanna was exploring her inner feelings about her cancer. Her thoughts follow.

Journey to within

My experience of having cancer is, and has been, one of the most intense periods of my life. The experience of having cancer has forced me to look at, to explore and to change myself in a way that no other experience in my life has done. Now I find myself wanting to write about that experience. Why?

Now that I am apparently 'all right' again, I find myself in danger of slipping into old patterns. The period of 'having cancer', especially the time when I was deeply involved in doing the Gerson therapy, was a time of immense intensity and, I felt, of great self-awareness, brought about by the necessity of 'living in the moment' that the diet imposed on me. Now, with that behind me, I am, as before, becoming more preoccupied with questions about 'what I shall do'. Yet I feel that that experience of 'being' was, is, invaluable to me. In writing about it, I will be focusing on it, turning my attention to it, once again. Writing is, for me, an act of 'remembering' (what, exactly, do I mean by that?), of reminding myself of the value of 'being', of living in the 'now'.

My journey has been greatly and constantly facilitated by my work with two psychosynthesis therapists, and indeed without their help and support I do not feel that my journey would or could have led me to where I am today – to a place of great physical vitality and, most importantly, a place where I feel a renewed urge to go forward with my life, despite the pains, disappointments and setbacks of the past. I am convinced that illness, especially life-threatening illnesses such as cancer, very often comes because there is some deeply fundamental change that is seeking to take place in ourselves and our lives. Sadly, very often the shock and threat of the illness itself is such that people are overtaken by it. If, however, a person can be, as I was, supported from the outset of the illness, then there can be the opportunity for the needed change and growth to take place. So often, however, the barriers to this happening prove insurmountable: the barriers of fear, guilt, feelings of inadequacy, self-distrust or self-hate. This latter is one of the greatest stumbling blocks – the feeling that, to get an illness such as cancer, there must be something deeply 'wrong with me'. One of the most important functions of the therapist is to provide 'unconditional love'. If I can reveal all the things about myself that I find most difficult, that I most dislike and despise, and still be accepted and loved, then there is a good chance that I can come to accept and love myself as well, despite all my failings. For it is well known that people who get cancer are often great perfectionists who set, at times, impossibly high standards for themselves.

Much has been written about the physical causes of cancer, and the physical treatments that can offer a cure. There is far less information about the psychological factors that may contribute to an individual developing cancer, and even less about the psychological help that many cancer sufferers undoubtedly need. If, as some doctors and health practitioners now believe, stress is a major contributory factor, then many people who develop cancer may be in need of psychological help and support for problems and issues that have been present in their lives for some time. Indeed, looking at and resolving these difficulties may enable an individual to have a lot more psychological energy available to mobilise towards their recovery. In his book *Love, Medicine and Miracles*, Bernie Siegel describes how one patient disliked the idea of using visualisation in an aggressive way, and pictured his white cells carrying away the cancer cells. This approach certainly resonated with me, and I found part of my visualisation developing in the following way.

Each time I breathed in and took oxygen into my body, little lights on my white cells – rather like the lamps on miners' helmets – lit up and showed them where any cancer cells were. The white cells then carried the cancer cells away. Next I watched the white cells emerging from a black tunnel and depositing all the cancer cells in a pile outside. There a strong sun was shining brightly, which, in time, dried out the cancer cells, shrivelling them up so that only husks remained.

Joanna was very upset by the publication of the Lancet *report, and wrote a letter to the* Guardian *after the screening by BBC2 on 14 September 1990 of* The Cancer Question, *which reinforced the damage done to the Cancer Help Centre by the publication of the report the previous week. The letter, hitherto unpublished, is given below.*

The Cancer Question: another patient's view

Is cancer a 'problem' to be 'solved', or one of life's mysteries that by its nature is compelling many people – patients and their loved ones, doctors, nurses and those practising complementary therapies – along challenging paths of doubt, self-discovery, pain and joy, a deeper appreciation of self and others and of the possible meaning that life could hold for us?

I believe it is the latter. Three years ago my breast cancer was diagnosed and, since then, I have undertaken a range of both orthodox and complementary medical treatment. This included a one-day visit to the Bristol Cancer Help Centre. That visit gave me three very important things:

- hope;
- confidence in my own ability to make decisions about what treatment I felt was right for me;
- an introduction to healing, which has been a great support.

Since that time, I have felt very fortunate in receiving wonderful treatment and support from many people, both doctors practising orthodox medicine and those engaged in complementary approaches.

I was flabbergasted when I watched the second part of *The Cancer Question* on BBC 2 at the vitriolic attacks some members of the medical profession were making, both on Penny Brohn personally and on the Cancer Help Centre, especially the diet. Dr Lesley Fallowfield, in particular, spoke bitterly of a patient of hers who lay dying, 'orange with the effects of carrot juice' and greatly distressed because she had 'failed with the diet'.[1]

This may be so, but as an ex-nurse, I have nursed many patients who were also deeply distressed at the effects radiotherapy or chemotherapy had had upon them. Or, indeed, so affected by these treatments that they no longer 'felt' anything much at all.

Attempts such as these to apportion 'blame' are of little use to anyone, especially us patients. Cancer is a disease that arouses many very strong feelings. Anger is one of them. I have felt a lot of anger as a patient and I believe that many doctors also experience deep anger when cancer claims yet another life of one of the patients for whom they have cared and for whom they feel responsible.

This anger, on the part of both patients and doctors, needs to be acknowledged. If it is not acknowledged and accepted as part of the often very unpalatable process, then it will continue to be misdirected at perceived 'outsiders' – the Bristol Cancer Help Centre and patients who dare to 'deviate' from medically acceptable forms of treatment. And it is, and will be, patients who suffer. And if I, as so many cancer patients do, was facing my death, whom would I choose to have with me, to be with me? Not an angry doctor or one who felt, perhaps unconsciously, 'guilty' at their 'failure' to prolong my life.

I was fortunate to be able to touch on these subjects with my ex- (and still greatly missed) GP. She told me of a cancer patient of hers who had been rushed several hundred miles, under some stress, for additional treatment which could have been offered locally. He died soon after his arrival at the other hospital. In retrospect my GP felt that he would have benefited more from staying where he was and being supported and helped to face his imminent death.

When I walked through that doctor's door, she inevitably greeted me with the words, 'What have you found out about that you've got to tell me this time?' Although she was extremely anxious for me to have radiotherapy following my initial surgery, she was able to tolerate my doubts and indecision and support my exploration of complementary avenues. I did eventually decide to have a course of radiotherapy. She is someone whom I would welcome with me if I was dying.

So, yes, it is about quality of treatment, of life, of acceptance and support. It is also about doubt, anger, guilt and despair. When I have been supported in recognising and expressing those feelings, I have at times experienced great joy and a deep sense of the fullness of life.

I have seen two counsellors/therapists since the beginning of my illness, and it has mainly been in my work with them that I have been able to explore and experience the feelings I have just described. For me, getting cancer has led me into a deeper exploration of myself, my life and my feelings than ever before. I have felt that I not only need to look at my immediate life situation and all the feelings that that arouses, but also at many issues from the past, and my often unrecognised and unexpressed feelings about these.

We live in a time when science is throwing much light on many things, and making important new discoveries. This includes the field of medicine, where life-saving drugs and new procedures are to be welcomed. But let us not forget that with each new light of discovery and understanding comes the corresponding darkness of yet further areas of unknowing, uncertainty and mystery. To deny that, to focus only on the 'problem-solving' and to forget the mystery, doubt and uncertainty is, to me, to deny a vital and ever-present part of life.

We all, patients, their loved ones, doctors and everyone involved with cancer, need not only to seek the answers to this disease but also to live our lives along the paths of the many questions it raises. Blaming each other for perceived failure will not, I believe, bring us any closer to the answers we seek.

Note

1   Joanna was quoting from memory. What Dr Fallowfield actually said was that she had anecdotes to suggest that the diet was 'positively harmful'. 'I think burned on my memory banks for ever will be the sight of a seriously emaciated young woman dying from breast cancer, tinged orange from the vast quantities of carrot juice she'd had to drink, really depressed and very distressed about the fact that her demise was due to the fact that she hadn't found the diet easy to stick to.' *The Cancer Question*, BBC 2, 14 September 1990.

10 Never Say Die

Joan Ward

Joan lives in Sussex with her husband and young son. Since her original diagnosis in 1986 at the age of 41 she has advanced her career in teaching, adding a further degree to her qualifications: she is now a deputy headmistress. She took part in the television documentary *The Cancer War Story* in May 1995.

I was born in Birmingham in 1944. My father was a policeman and my mother a cake-shop assistant. My brothers, Barry and Brian, are ten and nine years older than me. It has only been in recent years that I have ceased to be embarrassed in my mother's company when she has announced that I was not a mistake. 'We went in for our Joan' was the given formula.

I was rather indulged as a child, particularly by my father, but I also developed an independence of spirit. This was probably a matter of necessity, given the age and sex of my siblings, but I also think that it can be attributed to fairly long periods spent on my own when my parents were working. This, and a certain built-in self-confidence, must have been a significant factor in my being appointed head girl in my last year at Swanshurst Girls' Grammar School. Apart from that honour, I had not had a brilliant school career. The local tennis club was the centre of my world in those days. I nevertheless gained the 'statutory' three A levels, but decided not to apply for university.

For reasons which I found difficult to articulate at the time, I had set my heart on a career as an officer in the WRAF. We had had no family tradition of military service. Indeed, my father did not serve during the war because he was a policeman; my older brother was not required to do national service because he was a science graduate at a time when these were in short supply; my younger brother became a conscientious objector and served the community as a hospital porter and by working in the parks department of Birmingham City Council.

I suppose that I was attracted by the apparent glamour of life in the forces, but I also knew that it would suit me very well to both live and work in the kind of isolated communities that RAF stations inevitably are. I received superb training in leadership and the development of my own personal qualities. My aptitude for service life was acknowledged when I was awarded the Sash of Merit at the end of my training. I am quite sure that the four years that I spent in the WRAF were responsible for my being shortlisted for every job that I subsequently applied for.

Senior officers were kind enough to say that I would have had a very good career if I had remained in the service. The pull of married life was too great, however. My first marriage lasted seven years. We were well enough suited, but a childhood and youth spent in Kenya followed by years in the conviviality of officers' messes all over the world had given my husband a drinking problem. I was too young to know how to cope with it, or even to give it a name. I only know that there were many occasions on which I was desperately unhappy without any apparent means of help.

I tried to forge a life for myself by becoming a mature student at St Luke's College, Exeter. After four years of being a housewife in isolated areas, the life at college was wonderful. I spent the weekdays in Exeter and went home to Cornwall at the weekends. I was very highly motivated and my brain was enjoying the intellectual stimulus. College had also become an escape from my personal troubles. My final year at college saw a divorce and remarriage and a move from a luxurious lifestyle to the virtual poverty of being married to a fellow student. Miraculously, at the end of this year I gained a first class honours degree in Music and Philosophy, winning the university prize for gaining the top marks in my year. It had become apparent to me that I had developed the ability to concentrate my mind and to prioritise effectively despite extraordinary pressures.

I was appointed to the music staff of a large comprehensive school in Crawley. My innate self-confidence stood me in very good stead in surviving those first few years. In fact, I was promoted to head of department in only my second year of teaching. I would like to say that I was surprised by my meteoric rise but, looking back on it, I can only remember feeling that I was ready for the challenge. After five years of marriage, my husband and I divorced very amicably. This time, I was alone. Part of me regretted the loss of a partner; the other rather savoured the freedom that this new estate gave me.

I decided to take on a new challenge. Given my background in the Administrative Branch of the WRAF, I decided to apply for posts as an academic administrator. Terms of employment differ from those in the teaching profession. I therefore had to take the very risky step of resigning my teaching post before being appointed to an administrative one. The gamble paid off, however. I became the school administrator at the School of Adult and Community Studies, Goldsmiths College. These years also marked a return to a state of poverty.

I had taken a significant drop in salary, the train fare to New Cross Gate was crippling and the mortgage on the flat I had bought was almost too much for me to bear. My life was going to work and coming home. The year was 1980 and I had only £24 on which to keep myself for the month after the mortgage and loan for my season ticket had been paid. I had some lovely colleagues and friends, however. Despite the difficulties, my life was rich.

In July 1981 I met the man who was to become my third husband. My financial position had not improved. Indeed, I had had to sell my lovely baby grand piano; but I didn't yet know this man well enough to confide in him. I decided to relieve myself of the burden of paying for a season ticket – by buying a motorbike! Not for me some delicate Honda Melody. Oh no. I bought, for my first motorbike ever, a Honda CB 200 with full fairing. I learnt to ride it, or at least stay on it, in a weekend, and on Monday morning set off on the one-and-a-half-hour journey from Horsham to New Cross. I must have used up a lifetime's supply of adrenaline at that time. I did the whole distance for only three weeks. I did Coulsdon/New Cross return for a further 18 months. Black, wet winter nights were the worst, when the raindrops on the screen obscured my view of the road for several yards ahead. That terrifying adventure came to an end when I was three months pregnant with my first and only child.

I had never had particularly strong maternal feelings. There is no doubt that the absence of children had made the various changes in my life a lot easier to bear and to handle. Here I was though, nearly 39 years old and very glad to be pregnant. I had never been particularly ambitious either, so I felt no tension about being at home. In fact I savoured it, despite having a baby who sensed the moment I was dropping off on one of my attempted midday dozes. It was called 'demand' feeding! Despite the exhaustion of these times, life was good and happy. I had a lovely child and a husband who, though quiet, was a great family anchorman. My strong personality and extrovert nature he has never seen as a threat or something to be competed with. All those complex things that I am, are allowed to be.

After a year or so at home with Peter, I started to do some supply teaching. It was a perfect way of combining family responsibilities with a return to teaching. I soon confined my work to one particular school, St Wilfrid's, where I built up lasting friendships with superb colleagues. I had been working there for about two years when the biggest challenge of my life so far presented itself.

It was July 1986, and I went to a routine family planning appointment at my doctor's surgery in Horsham, West Sussex. It was two months before my forty-second birthday. I had been married four years and our son was three years old.

The nurse asked if I would like her to examine my breasts. I was pleased to accept her offer. Self-examination had always been unsatisfactory because my breasts were what I would describe as naturally lumpy. She paused during her examination of the right breast and explained that she would like the doctor himself to feel the tissue. My doctor arrived. He is a lovely man and I had been his patient for six years. He said that he could feel some granular tissue and that he thought it would be best if I had a mammogram. He said that I should not be troubled and that the test was simply a precaution. I certainly took that attitude myself and, when the appointment arrived for the first week in September, I didn't mind the delay.

At that time the nearest mammography unit was in Guildford. It was the first time that I had had such a test and I found it extremely uncomfortable, although I remember feeling grateful that examinations like that were available.

Less than a week later, I was in the kitchen preparing my son's tea when my doctor telephoned. He has a steady, gentle way, and he used this to explain that the radiologists were not happy with an area of tissue. The advice was that I should be admitted to Crawley Hospital, where I would be given a biopsy in order that the exact nature of the tissue could be discovered.

I went to hospital on 13 October and was asked to sign a form giving authority to the surgeon to perform further surgery, should it be considered necessary. I was happy to do that, partly because I didn't, in my heart, believe that it would come to that.

Nevertheless, I was relieved when I woke up in the recovery room to discover that I still had two breasts. A chunk of tissue the size of my index finger and the one next to it had been removed and I had a vertical scar with nine stitches in under the nipple. The surgeon visited the ward on the following day and explained that all was well. There had simply been a hardening of the tissue, probably attributable to changes in the balance of my hormones. I left hospital with a light heart and with an appointment for two weeks later.

I arrived for that appointment, imagining that it was simply a question of checking that the wound had healed well. A locum consultant walked in breezily and stood by me as he read my notes. As he read, he took a step back. Instinct told me that I should steel myself for what he had to say. He was putting distance between himself and me in preparation for imparting difficult news. Further tests had shown that there was malignancy in the breast. I should return the following week, when my own consultant would have returned from leave. End of consultation. I left the room and felt as if I stumbled past women I had been chatting to cheerily as we waited. I managed a strangled word but the lump in my throat was filling it.

My son was at a childminder's. My mind was in turmoil. I couldn't trust myself to be calm and collected. I got into the car and started to drive. As I negotiated traffic lights and roundabouts, I conceived the idea of going straight to a friend's house. She was in. She had another friend with her. I started to try to tell her but my throat just gave up and the tears started to fall. I sat on the settee, having my hands held each side. It relieved a lot of pressure. She phoned the childminder and warned her not to ask me how I had got on when I went to pick my son up. She spoke to my husband at work. His boss kindly drove him home. When I had calmed down and spent all the present tears, I went to pick up Peter. The childminder's eyes were kind and spoke volumes. The little boy was oblivious to the turmoil in his mother.

As we drove home, I responded to news of the afternoon's happening with my heart breaking. With two failed childless marriages behind me, I had a lovely husband and a cherished son. I didn't have a firm religious belief. The stark reminder of my mortality hurt. Who would take care of my son? How would my values be transmitted to him? He wouldn't remember me. That hurt the most. I wanted desperately to be an important factor in his life for many more years. As I write, it is nine years later and the tears begin again.

The charade of normality in front of the little one persisted when my husband came home. Despair filled me. I had so much to live for. I didn't want to be cheated. A kind of fighting spirit emerged. I started to feel that death might not be inevitable. I was rational and composed when I saw the consultant a week later. I knew that he would recommend a mastectomy. He had two reasons. One was that it had not proved 'feasible' to remove the whole area of granular tissue. The other had to do with the type of breast cancer that I had. Apparently, there are several different kinds. The sort that I had affects the lining of the milk ducts and a characteristic of this kind of cancer is that it can produce tumours in more than one place within the breast.

I had two weeks to wait before being readmitted to hospital. The feeling of wanting to help myself and take some control over the fight to help me live persisted. Throughout my life, books had been an important source of knowledge and it was to these that I turned. I discovered, quite by chance, Penny Brohn's book *Gentle Giants*. I was at once riveted and excited by it. It spoke of the ways in which we can help ourselves by detoxifying our systems, thereby giving the body's own immune system the chance to aid the process of healing. The whole thing made such sense. I read with delight about the way in which some people's cancer had been put in remission. I remember feeling 'How wonderful!' I also remember realising that this was not a claim. It was simply a demonstration of the way in which apparent miracles can sometimes happen. Some years later I had the opportunity to thank Penny for that inspiration and, indeed, to express some sorrow at the fact that, under tremendous subsequent pressure, Bristol had felt forced to deny the possibility of healing. It had seemed to me, and still appears to be, a commonsensical proposition that a healthy body will house within it the means to aid the healing process. Today, few would deny that.

My mother had come down from Birmingham. I had organised a rota of my friends to bring Mum and Peter to the hospital to visit me on weekday afternoons. Despite the charade and the cheery words of explanation, when the time came for my husband to take me to hospital, my son evidently understood the nature of the wrench. He did not, however, cling to me as I said 'Goodbye.' I could not have borne that. Instead he turned and went and held my mother's leg. In that instant, he had transferred the source of his security. I had never before, or since, felt such a depth of bleakness, and yet even this seemed to say, 'I won't ask anything of you at the moment. Save all your strength to make yourself better.'

The operation included the taking of samples from the lymph glands in my armpit. If they were clear, all would be well. If they were not, I would need radio- and chemotherapy. I settled into the routine of hospital life. The dressing around my chest was so bulky that the difference in my figure wasn't at all evident. Then the day came for the dressing to be removed. The nurse was sensitive and kind. She warned me that women quite often cry when they see themselves for the first time. I remember being fascinated rather than despairing at the sight of my new self. Life was my priority now. There was no energy to waste on regret.

The follow-up appointment was ten days after leaving hospital. I would also hear the results of the lymph gland sampling. This time my husband came with me. We steeled ourselves as we waited. We were ushered in. When it came, it was brief, casual and almost dismissive. 'Well, the tests were clear. You won't need any further treatment.' To the consultant, it was all in an afternoon's work. To me, it was a return to the world, but this time in glorious technicolour and stereophonic sound. I had looked the possibility of death in the face and had, on this occasion, denied it. I had learnt an important lesson, though. I had discovered a way and a group of people who would tell me how to help myself to stay fit; who would give me confidence that I could take responsibility for important aspects of my own health. I had an appointment to visit the Bristol Cancer Help Centre on 6 January 1987 and I was going to keep it.

I was introduced to a new world – a world that I hadn't moved in before. I knew that several new and strange things would be on offer: relaxation, healing, counselling and advice about diet. I wasn't nervous. My heart and mind were open to anything which would keep me fit and help me stay alive. Any nerves were instantly dispelled when we arrived at Bristol. The homeliness of the atmosphere and the humility with which advice and therapies were offered were immediately impressive. I was in the hands of people I could trust and believe in.

While I was at Bristol, it was explained to me that a study was about to begin in which the survival rates and quality of life of women who had been to Bristol were to be compared with those of women who had not visited the Centre. I was asked if I would contribute to this study by agreeing to fill in a questionnaire once a year over the next four years. I agreed without hesitation.

I remember being very disappointed when, a few weeks later, the first questionnaire arrived. It was simplistic and only seemed to scrape the surface of what Bristol had meant to me. I nevertheless filled it in as fully as I could and, indeed, did so with a further two identical forms. Imagine my amazement and disgust when a few months later I was sitting watching the news on TV with my husband. The newscaster read: 'Recent research has shown that women who have been to Bristol are twice as likely to die as women who have not.' Could this possibly refer to the research of which I had been a part? If it did, how could the researchers have possibly reached those conclusions on the miserable evidence of the questionnaires and after so little time?

In a sense, the rest of that is now well-known history. Bristol seemed inexplicably silent. I was quite certain that they would emerge, like knights in shining armour, refuting the findings of the research team, but there was nothing. Fortunately, women with more skill, time and energy than I had formed a group of which I became a small part. The Bristol Survey Support Group proved to be a formidable force. Its voice was heard in influential places by important people. The whole question of the ethics of medical research was put under the microscope.

There are many people who know a lot more about the details of the whole affair than I do, but I do have an opinion about the status of the researchers' report. I realise that it is in the nature of scientific research that scientists produce hypotheses, and to these they attach the best evidence available to them at the time. The world moves on and scientific knowledge increases. New researchers come along who are able to add to, or amend, the body of knowledge in any given area of research. I remain convinced, however, that what happened here is a fundamentally different question. Several aspects of the report have been found to be flawed. The authors themselves have acknowledged this. The research has no scientific value in my eyes and the report should be withdrawn.

While the battle over the report has been raging, my life has moved on. For the first five years following my operation, I was glad to be alive, regardless of the shape of my body. I patiently coped with a prosthesis and became adept at wearing as near normal clothes as I could. Evening wear was quite a challenge.

Evidence of cleavage with evening wear was not easily achieved, despite my most ingenious efforts!

As the years passed and the possibility of a recurrence receded, I began to think that I didn't want to have to spend the rest of my life confined to certain styles of dress or having to put my hand to my chest each time I bent down in a summer dress. The idea of having an implant became attractive. After quite a long wait, it was my turn. The operation itself proved more uncomfortable and difficult to get over than the original mastectomy. It was, however, well worth it. The nightmare of nine years ago seems a long way off.

Throughout this time, my friends at St Wilfrid's were a wonderful source of support. Their compassionate acceptance of the new 'me' made the task of recovery so much easier. As months turned into years, I began to look to the future of my professional life too. I had my part-time schoolteaching, a small private piano-teaching practice, and I had found time to become a voluntary associate working with the probation service. I felt that now was the time to attempt an MA in English Literature. Music had given me a good start in my career, but it was English that I wanted to spend the rest of my life teaching. Sussex University had accepted me on the course and I had my life reasonably organised to cope with it, when St Wilfrid's asked me to teach full-time during the following year. I couldn't bear to give up the chance of starting the MA. So for that first year I worked full-time, gave private piano lessons and did the course. The only concession I made concerned the voluntary work with the probation service. Instead of spending time doing work locally, I undertook to write letters to people in prison. This presented a challenge all of its own. My clients included murderers and a woman who had been convicted of aiding and abetting the rape of children.

The reader may well be wondering where Peter fitted into all these activities. The answer is that, at that time, he was at a boarding school. Such a move had certainly not been part of our planning for him, but had come about quite naturally. At his first school I had made friends with a lady whose two older children boarded. I was given an insight into a world that I didn't know, but which I felt would suit Peter very much. Being the only child of older parents, we wanted him to know what it was like to live with other children and to savour moments of solitude rather than their being predominant in his life. Each parting was hard, but he took well to the life of being away from home.

At the time of my breast reconstruction operation in 1992, it had become apparent that the local management of schools had produced funding problems which meant that it was becoming more and more difficult for St Wilfrid's to employ me. This coincided with the deepest years of the present recession. My husband is a photographer. He has worked for the same company for 24 years. It did not escape the general tightening and so assured annual pay rises were no longer possible.

I therefore decided to try to return to full-time teaching. While I was waiting for an appropriate post to present itself, I saw an advertisement for tutor counsellors with the Open University. I made an application and was interviewed. I was told that it would be six to eight weeks before the OU could let me know the result. In the meantime, the possibility of an excellent post had presented itself. This was as a full-time English teacher at an independent, coeducational day school in Worthing. Once again, cruel timing put me under tremendous pressure. The OU finally offered me a part-time post, but wanted me to sign the contract with some haste. This was four days before the interview for the job in Worthing. I could certainly not assume that that application would be successful and so I signed the contract. Four days later I was offered, and very gladly accepted, the teaching post.

There then followed two years of full-time English teaching, with all the marking that that entails, the continuation of piano lessons, and the OU work which took up one evening fortnightly for study sessions and one weekend in three for marking. It was extremely hard, but the move to Worthing had been just the right thing for me. Our Lady of Sion is a lovely school. It was the nearest thing that I had experienced to my old grammar school – and I thought that such schools had disappeared. As each day passed, I thought 'Peter would like this. This is just the sort of education that he needs.' My husband and I decided that Peter should leave his boarding school and begin his secondary school career at Sion. I remain convinced that his three years' boarding was time very well spent and achieved the ends that we had aimed at in sending him away. It is wonderful, of course, to have him back with us all the time. We are pleased that we shall be on hand as Peter progresses through adolescence, hopefully being able to guide his thoughts and reactions to the trials of growing up.

Shortly before Peter moved to Our Lady of Sion, the school's deputy head gave notice that she was to retire the following Christmas, after ten years in post. My immediate instinct was to apply for the post, although I realised that it might seem an impertinent application in some ways. I was not even a head of department and I had not long returned to full-time teaching. I had, however, once been a head of department in a very large school and I did have experience as an academic administrator. Suffice it to say that I did apply and that my application was successful.

As I have said, I have never been particularly ambitious, but I now find myself, with ten years left to work, in the privileged position of filling a post which gives me a tremendous 'buzz'. It is almost as if the whole of my life has led me to this point. All the talents that I was dealt and the experience I have gained along the way can be put to use in this thriving school community. Although my husband and my headmaster are very different characters, they have one very important thing in common. Neither of them feels threatened by me or resentful of what I am. Each gives me the space that I need to produce the best that is in me. Not a day passes without my rejoicing in my good fortune. Would my life have been different, I wonder, if I had not had to cope with cancer? I do believe that nature had already endowed me with a character and personality which made the struggle against a life-threatening disease easier to cope with, but I shall be eternally grateful for the Bristol Cancer Help Centre.

The things I learnt there in 1987, I hear from many varied sources now. It made sense to me then and it still does now. It is very important to me that Bristol survives and that women who have to face their own nightmares can be given the same hope and enabling capacity that I found there. The experience of a life-threatening disease is at once sobering and enriching. Sometimes we need help to ensure that we can tap into that means of enrichment.

11 The Search for Meaning

Heather Young*

Before her diagnosis of cancer in 1986 at the age of 55, Heather had spent most of her working life as an academic editor. Her visit to the Cancer Help Centre led to a change of career: she now works as a counsellor.

Where does my story start? What was it in my family history or background that made me cancer-prone?

First, I come from a 'cancer family', particularly on my father's side. My father, grandfather and one aunt died from bowel cancer, another aunt and paternal grandmother from breast cancer. My mother died of Parkinson's Disease, but her mother died of breast cancer when her only child, my mother, was nine years old. So both grandmothers died of breast cancer in their fifties.

It is hardly surprising, moreover, that I developed the characteristics of the so-called 'cancer-prone personality'.[1] I was born in 1931, and a fortnight after my birth my father returned to West Africa, where he worked for the Church Missionary Society (CMS), leaving my mother alone with me. She told me later that she was frightened of me: she was scared of dropping me, as if I were a china doll; she had no experience of babies, and brought me up by the book – the 'bible' in those days being the work of the paediatrician Truby King, who advised four-hourly feeds, no more and no less, on the dot. No wonder I sucked frantically for comfort: not my thumb but my nightie. The result was prominent teeth which became an orthodontist's nightmare during the troubled war years when we always seemed to be on the move.

---

* I had not originally intended to contribute a chapter about my own experiences, but it seemed unfair to expect others to write their stories and not be brave enough to do so myself. So by reverting to my maiden name I am able to bring up the rear in this alphabetically arranged series of chapters, and to draw some threads together in a coda. – Heather Goodare, née Young.

After 18 months of virtual single motherhood my mother decided she had to join my father, taking me with her. This was considered very risky (apparently I was the first white child to be taken to West Africa), but I survived two bouts of malaria before the age of five, when I was packed off to the CMS boarding school in England. By this time my younger brother was a toddler, and his life followed much the same pattern.

At the time I settled down well at school in Surrey: the kindergarten was a happy place and I had a motherly teacher. Together with my aunt in Yorkshire, where I went during the school holidays, she provided the love that I lacked from my own mother. How could my mother love me? She just wasn't there. My father, on the other hand, though absent, sent me delightful letters in rhyme with little drawings down the margin: he was a talented artist, with a warm personality. I wrote letters to my parents dutifully every Sunday, as instructed. But they were remote figures.

This upbringing ensured that I was well-behaved, obedient, compliant. In order to earn my parents' love I *had* to excel at school. It was too dangerous to show feelings. I don't remember my mother ever praising me. If I did well, I ought to have done better. I only saw my parents every 18 months during these early years, so they were inevitably strangers when we did meet. I was much closer to my aunt, who was fun to be with and had a creative streak: she wrote poetry and put on nativity plays in the church, which I remember taking part in.

I cannot blame my mother: she did her best for us children. Her own personality had of course been shaped by *her* family history: the death of her mother when she was nine, and the subsequent alcoholism of her father. The only way she could survive was by being fiercely independent, a quality she carried to the end of her life.

When the war came my mother decided she should remain in Britain to be near us, while my father continued to travel backwards and forwards in convoy to Sierra Leone. Once again she was isolated, living in a series of bedsitting rooms and flats, before she found a cottage near my aunt in Yorkshire. Then at the age of 11-plus I was entered for the 'bluecoat school', Christ's Hospital, and my brother for the preparatory department. As children of missionaries on low salaries we qualified for more-or-less free places. But in that era, during wartime, Christ's Hospital was a singularly bleak establishment, and I was now separated from my brother, who went to the boys' school at Horsham while I went to the girls' school at Hertford. Academically the school was excellent, with small classes, a good library and laboratories, and even a domestic science department with a furnished flat attached. But the House – or Ward as it was called – was a comfortless place, with tiny lockers where each girl could keep her few possessions, and a harsh regime. I learnt to survive and, again, how to repress my feelings.

One of my few opportunities to escape from this world was through music. I had a good singing voice and had sung in school choirs from early days. I also learnt the violin, and at the age of 16 became a founder member of the newly formed National Youth Orchestra (NYO). I shall never forget the audition, in Dinelys Studios in Baker Street, where I had gone in my Sunday best – the school coat-frock, an unbecoming garment. Miss Railton, now Dame Ruth, on hearing me play, said: 'Christ's Hospital, I knew it! You're all inhibited and repressed! Play it again, child.' I played the piece again with what I hoped was a little more abandon, and she said: 'My dear, I feel so sorry for you, I must have you in my orchestra.' I shall be eternally grateful to Ruth Railton for taking pity on me. I went on to lead the second violins, and spent wonderful holidays learning great music with great musicians, visiting magical places like Paris, Aberdeen, Edinburgh, Brighton, Bath.

At Christ's Hospital the compliant, hardworking, conscientious person that I had become was rewarded by my appointment as head girl. But the National Youth Orchestra was nurturing the rebellious, nonconformist, spiritually adventurous side of me, and I think the headmistress got more than she bargained for in her head girl. Without the NYO my life would have been very dull. With it, my rough edges were smoothed and I arrived at Oxford university with at least the bare minimum of social graces.

My years there reading English from 1949 to 1952 were rich and fascinating. We were full of postwar idealism and didn't mind the continued rationing. My father had returned home at the end of the war and now had a job in London. Family holidays included sailing on the Norfolk Broads: my brother had taught himself sailing from the books of Arthur Ransome, and my father graciously conceded on our first morning on the River Bure that John, not he, was the family expert. I too came to love sailing. After leaving school my brother emigrated to New Zealand and finally settled in Australia.

I had ambitions to enter publishing, but the only way in for a girl was through secretarial work. A small endowment policy that my grandfather had bought for me at birth matured when I was 21, so I cashed it in and took a postgraduate secretarial course in Oxford. I only worked for a short time as a secretary before becoming an editor in educational publishing. Years later my boss, Alan Hill, in his autobiography *In Pursuit of Publishing*,[2] after some generous remarks about my work, added:

> Above all she was the keeper of the conscience of HEB [Heinemann Educational Books]. Where some business decision conflicted with moral principle, she would unhesitatingly denounce the person concerned face to face – not excepting myself, to whom she once applied the epithet 'humbug.'

Looking back, I must have been the most awful prig.

This work satisfied my creativity (I became interested in typography and book production), used my English degree and felt worthwhile, until after eight years I found myself clashing with Alan over African politics. My father had worked in West Africa and I knew something of the background. I left Heinemann in 1964.

During my time at Heinemann I met and married my first husband, who was a refugee from Eastern Europe. He was handsome, warm, volatile, romantic, above all *different* from the rather pale young men I had encountered at Oxford. He appreciated the arts with an intensity born of long frustration under Communist censorship. Moreover, he wooed me with an un-English passion that totally swept me off my feet. I still couldn't really believe that anyone could think me *worthy* of love. Nobody had loved me like that before. I had never been good enough or clever enough for my mother. I was very self-conscious about my still-prominent teeth, but they didn't seem to worry my husband. He encouraged my good points, helped me to dress well (though we had little money), gave me a confidence in my own abilities that I had never before possessed. In return, of course I helped him with his English (when we first met we had spoken French to each other, our only common language) and with finding his way around the labyrinthine British system, with its many unwritten rules. I adored him, but in retrospect perhaps there was something lacking on my part: some ultimate inhibition that I couldn't quite shed. He was also a little younger than me, and as he was a stranger in a foreign country I tended to assume responsibility for things that in other partnerships might have been organised by the husband. When we married he was still a music student. When we parted he had made a name for himself as a musicologist.

After long years of infertility and many investigations I finally managed to conceive a child at the age of 38. My son was born when I was six months short of my fortieth birthday. It was for me a miraculous moment. As mature parents, we were going to be more sensible than most. What I had not reckoned with were the huge adjustments required to our lives by the late entry of this new member to our family. My son's birth was even more precious because he had been conceived after my husband had been successfully treated for cancer. This resurrection had been magically followed by new birth. We were both thrilled with our son. My husband had not been so determined on procreation as I was, but once the child was born he became almost obsessed with him: he nursed him, played with him, walked and talked with him, *enjoyed* him hugely. Since his operation he had been working part-time, and I kept the budget balanced by freelance editing, so he was able to spend more time with his son than most fathers do. It was a perfect partnership, an ideal modern marriage, with equal roles in parenting and providing. Or so I thought.

When my husband returned from lecturing at a summer school with clear signs that our relationship had changed, I was desolate. He had met a woman almost half my age, and been captivated by her. Throughout our marriage I had marvelled that my attractive husband had not (apparently) been tempted to stray, but I never seriously thought that he would do so after the birth of our son. I could understand him falling out of love with me – a middle-aged, tired mum with greying hair. But I couldn't understand how he could even think of leaving our child.

Leave us he did, after much heartbreak. My world fell apart, but I tried desperately to cling to some semblance of self-respect. My freelance editing was not enough to keep us afloat, so I had to find full-time work, and a nanny to look after my little boy, who was now nearly four years old. Somehow we survived. On the surface I coped quite well, holding down a responsible job. But underneath I felt the most black despair, and had to resort to sleeping pills. With my churchy background divorce was the ultimate failure. 'Be ye perfect' had been drummed into me since childhood. I had so wanted to be a perfect mother, and now this was impossible:

I had to leave my son with a nanny and commute to an office every day. Income tax rules at the time meant that I had no allowance for the nanny: if I had been a man in a similar situation, I would have qualified for one. My ex-husband, whose cancer had returned, was now in poor health and could contribute little. I was constantly worried about money. My nanny ran a car; I could ill afford a motorbike, which I rode 33 miles each way every day to get to work. Although I was eating heartily (my motorbike rides made me very hungry), I lost nearly 2 stone in weight, going from about 9 stone down to 7.

After two years I was offered another job nearer home, which carried with it a company car. This made life a lot easier. My son started school, and I no longer needed a nanny but could manage with an au pair. But at the same time my mother's health deteriorated and she came to live with me, now aged 74 and suffering from advanced Parkinson's Disease. She was not well enough to help with my son, needing help herself, which it was not fair to ask the au pair to provide. After a nightmarish few months during which she was in and out of hospitals and nursing homes, my brother came over from Australia and took her to live near him. The Australians at that time had a liberal immigration policy for dependent relatives, and she was well looked after until she died.

During this time, the only holiday I could afford was a week at a music camp nearby (taking my son and the au pair as well). This camp I had visited on and off since my early twenties, and it seemed a wonderfully safe refuge, with a chance to be myself again. I was certainly not thinking of new relationships, simply of playing my violin, and when I met again an old musical friend who was now in the same situation as me, having been left by his wife, with three teenage children, I was initially very reluctant to become involved. Getting to know each other was difficult as we lived 60 miles apart, on opposite sides of London. Slowly however we grew together, and the idea of remarriage began to make sense for both of us.

This second marriage was obviously quite different from the first. We were both middle-aged, both hurt, both seeking the healing of wounds. Neither could entirely fulfil the other's needs. In order to marry Ken I had to leave behind my job, my car, my house, my friends and my hard-won independence. I had to fit in with a new set of relationships and take on three teenage children. By the time of our marriage the two older ones had left school and were semi-independent, but the youngest was struggling with the damage done by his parents' break-up and (though he never said so) must have resented the entry of a younger child into the family, usurping his position as youngest.

While I had been on my own I could not afford the luxury of stopping to *feel* anything much: I just had to carry on somehow. Now for the first time since my first husband had left I was able to stop and not just think, but feel. These feelings turned out to be mixed. I was glad that I could give more time to my son, and my new stepchildren welcomed me warmly, but trying to heal all the hurts was too much for me: I had been too badly damaged myself. My new husband had many virtues, but his personality was the exact opposite of my former husband's: in a way this was one reason for marrying him, so it was totally illogical of me to want him to be any different. But underneath I had not properly grieved, and of course I could not really grieve anyway since the relationship had not ended: contact had to be maintained for the sake of our son, who needed to visit his father, speak to him on the phone and write to him.

If I couldn't be the perfect mother at least I was going to do a good job of mending our two muddled families. This was my aim; the reality was that whatever I achieved on the surface was at the cost of my own health. Physically I was now fine; I had regained normal weight. Emotionally I was drained, and still not sleeping properly. I went through bouts of severe depression. My GP was supportive, but could not change the situation that gave rise to my chronic stress. I was doing some desultory freelance editing and a little violin playing, but my life centred round the family and its complications. My younger stepson was still unhappy, and I felt I was failing to give him the right kind of support. Slowly I tried to make domestic improvements, but changing things was not easy and I became discouraged. I suffered from anxiety as well as depression. This took the form of panic attacks, sometimes in supermarkets, which was very embarrassing. I also found it difficult to make decisions. I couldn't post a letter without opening the envelope half a dozen times to check that the contents were correct. I couldn't leave the house without obsessively returning to check that I had turned off the oven, shut the back door, double-locked the front door and so on.

The menopause then added physical distress: backache, cramp, almost non-stop bleeding, with the humiliating onset of unexpected flooding in public places, and night sweats that made sleep even more difficult. My doctor tried various remedies before prescribing hormone replacement therapy (HRT), which gave me immediate relief from the physical symptoms but made little difference to my mental state. I felt isolated: I had left behind many of my closest women friends when I remarried, and I could find no one to confide in – except the anonymous Samaritans. I had never been one for the coffee-morning round, and lacked self-confidence as never before. I stopped going to church as it all seemed stuffy and pointless. I had no relations in the UK except my husband's family; all my own relations were dead or had emigrated. I felt thoroughly miserable, lonely and spiritually desolate.

However, things were to change. My brother came over with his wife from Australia during the summer of 1986. He stayed with us for a week, during which time I talked to him almost non-stop. I poured out all my feelings of guilt, frustration, bitterness, anger. He just listened, not commenting or judging. He had shared the same childhood, and knew without my having to tell him all the things that were important to us both. At the end of the week came his one and only attempt at confrontation. 'Y'know Heather, you bitch too much?' he said in his Australian drawl with its interrogative upturn at the end of the sentence, which somehow made it less threatening.

Of course he was absolutely right. But only he had earned the right to say that, because he had really *listened*. It seemed to me that I couldn't sink much lower in my self-pitying depression; perhaps it was time I tried to climb out of my black hole. Later that summer we went for a week's sailing holiday in Cornwall – my brother, sister-in-law, husband, son and myself. I had no responsibilities: my brother was looking after the boats, my sister-in-law was in charge of the cooking, my husband was doing the driving, my son (now aged 15) was being generally useful and I could concentrate on getting well. I was surrounded by people who loved me. At the beginning of the week I was still taking both anti-depressants and sleeping pills. By the end of it I was taking no pills, and feeling a lot happier and fitter, though still not sleeping very soundly. However, I persisted with my new routine and slowly sleep returned. I began to see that *I* was the person who had to change, not those around me.

During the autumn I started really enjoying life again. I started looking up old friends, including one in London who told me about her breast cancer and her visit to the Bristol Cancer Help

Centre. By chance I met a French nun living locally: she had lost her way back to her convent, and I helped her with a map and French conversation. We became firm friends and met many more times. I started going to church again; there had been a change of vicar and I now felt much more at home. Around this time I had a strange experience: a kind of vision in which I was a lost lamb, borne home on the shoulders of the good shepherd.

I was playing in the local orchestra again, and one evening after rehearsal I noticed a sharp pain in my right armpit: I simply thought I had overdone things during the rehearsal and had strained my bowing arm. But the next morning I was trying on a new bra, looking in the mirror to check the fit, when I noticed a dimpling to one side of the breast. I felt it, and to my horror found a large lump the size of a plum. How on earth had I not noticed it earlier? I can only think that after my years of depression I was now too busy enjoying life to worry about examining my breasts. I went straight down to my GP without even making an appointment, and waited till the end of surgery to see him. He tried to reassure me: 'Ninety per cent of these lumps are not malignant.' But he made an appointment for me to see a surgeon the very next day.

Still buoyed up by my doctor's reassurance, and feeling very fit, I was alarmed when the surgeon said: 'Yes, well, that lump will have to come out. I'm afraid the earliest I can manage is in a fortnight's time.' Why the hurry, I wondered. I asked him almost casually, 'Oh, do you think it's cancer?' and the reply was: 'As a matter of fact, yes I do, but I can't be certain until I operate.'

At that my knees turned to jelly and my brave new world collapsed. There was no breast care nurse, no Macmillan nurse, no cup of tea on offer. Not quite knowing what I was doing, I drove myself home. I left a note for my son, who was expected home from school at any minute, and found a neighbour to talk to. I knew nobody in my home town who had had breast cancer, but later that evening I rang my old friend in London. She recommended a visit to Bristol.

After the initial shock of the diagnosis, strangely enough, I did not relapse into depression. In a way it was easier to cope with a palpable physical illness than a nebulous depression, which few could understand or sympathise with. My long-suffering husband had been baffled by my Black Dog, and unable to help. Cancer by contrast was easier to cope with, and I found it evoked a lot more sympathy. When I had been depressed, there were many times when I *wanted* to die. Now I had cancer I very much wanted to live.

By the time I went into hospital I had obtained a copy of Penny Brohn's *Gentle Giants* and the literature about the Bristol Centre. I had even started to change my diet and take extra vitamin C. The more I read, the more it all seemed to make sense. Emotionally I had almost recovered from the years of anxiety and depression; but now it was the turn of my body to make its protest. During my depression I took poor care of myself: exercised little, ate junk food, drank too much coffee and alcohol, consumed large quantities of prescribed medication. The final pill had been HRT, which had undoubtedly helped with menopausal symptoms but probably increased the risk of breast cancer. My surgeon certainly thought so, and insisted that I came off it straight away. Strangely, when I did, my symptoms did not return.

Looking back, the pattern seemed clear: early separation from parents, an emotionally starved childhood, followed by a second emotional upheaval in adult life. It wasn't just my body that needed healing, it was my soul. My new friend Sister Jeanne seemed to understand, and came to visit me in hospital. The new vicar listened sympathetically to my tale of self-recrimination and guilt. By the time I went to the Bristol Centre with my husband in January 1987 I had already started on my self-help programme. Christmas meals had not been a problem, as my grown-up stepchildren were vegetarian and on their Christmas visit home introduced me to the mysteries of tofu and nut roasts: we even had fresh chestnuts from our own tree.

My 'head girl' characteristics had not entirely left me, however. I was anxious to do things correctly in relation to my orthodox clinicians, and asked for their blessing on my visit to Bristol. My GP was very supportive: he had seen me through my depression and thought the Centre sounded just what he would have ordered. Some details in the medical form for Bristol needed my consultant's attention, so along I went to the clinic and asked if she would fill them in. I was keen to have her approval too. Her words were: 'I don't mind if you go to Bristol and stain yourself yellow with carrot juice, my dear.' But she was insistent that the day after I came back I was to start radiotherapy.

At Bristol what we heard made perfect sense. In a strange way my healing had already started six months earlier, when my brother had stayed with us and had given me a whole week of loving listening. This had enabled me to climb out of my slough of despond. That I only found my breast lump three months later was immaterial – in fact providential, since by then I had acquired enough emotional strength to cope with it. The Cancer Help Centre simply confirmed me in the path I had already chosen: one of recovery from helplessness and hopelessness as a way of life, and discovery of all that still lay ahead of me.

As a consequence of my brother's visit I took on a fundraising job for a sail training project, the building of a topsail schooner, the *One and All*, in South Australia. The ship needed equipment that could only be obtained in the UK, and I undertook to arrange this, but there was still a financial deficit to be made up. When on the Sunday after Christmas a visiting preacher in our local church gave a sermon whose theme was the brave little trading schooners plying back and forth across the Atlantic in the last century I could hardly believe my ears. The *One and All* was that very day awaiting news that finance would be forthcoming to provide the final fitting out. Two days later I had a call from my brother in Adelaide to say that an anonymous donor had stepped in with A\$30,000 to bridge the gap. The ship, it seemed, was saved. The preacher's message was that we as Christians should launch forth into the New Year with all canvas set, however hard it was blowing: we should follow a high-risk strategy and not scuttle into harbour in a frightened huddle. This sermon reinforced my feeling that I was on the right track. I had a strange sense of being guided, even manipulated by a divine puppet-master. This was in startling contrast to my life for the previous five years, which had seemed to be one long muddle.

By the time my husband and I went to the Cancer Help Centre for a day in mid-January 1987 I was open to anything they had to offer. With their help I devised my personal 'get-well' programme. My husband too gained immensely from the visit, though on the face of it he was the last person to be impressed by anything 'alternative', being a man for logic and hard science. During that first year I returned for day visits half a dozen times, but (to my regret) never allowed myself the luxury of a whole week. By the following year I was attending seminars at the Centre for support group leaders and playing a part in the development of my local cancer self-help group.

Looking back at some notes I made at the time of my first visit to Bristol, I find the words:

If I could conquer depression, cancer can hold no terror for me.

> No more be grieved at that which thou hast done:
> Roses have thorns, and silver fountains mud;
> Clouds and eclipses stain both moon and sun,
> And loathsome canker lives in sweetest bud.
> All men make faults ...

Shakespeare's sonnet expresses it perfectly.

What the sonnet expressed for me was the feeling that I had now done enough grieving, that regrets were now pointless and that I was now allowed *not* to be perfect. I had finally grown up. Even the cancer was something natural, to be found in the animal and plant world: no big deal. One of my worst moments had been summoning up the courage to tell my son of my diagnosis; but for him, cancer was not a death sentence, since he knew that his father had had it and survived. He did not seem to be unduly worried by my cancer, though he made sure that he was the first to greet me with flowers when I came round from the anaesthetic – rushing out of school to be there as soon as possible.

I sailed through my radiotherapy treatment, armed with visualisation techniques learnt at Bristol. I enjoyed the recommended diet, which I am sure helped to mitigate the side effects of the treatment. I continued to play my violin (which helped with both physical and emotional rehabilitation). After the treatment ended I resumed work as a freelance editor. In fact I felt so well that I took on too much, and became anxious and depressed. Fearful of a relapse (into depression, not cancer), I consulted my GP. 'Have you been doing your relaxation and meditation?' he asked. I had to admit that I had let it slip. 'Well, there's no point in going to Bristol and not following the programme,' he said somewhat tartly. He prescribed a week off work and an outing to the sea. This trip was a visit to Portsmouth: I had been invited aboard one of the Australian bicentenary 'Re-enactment' fleet of tall ships about to set sail for Sydney (the *One and All*, my brother's brainchild, was one of them, and I had actually thought of forgoing this great pleasure because of my misplaced sense of duty to my work). My husband and I went to Portsmouth and had a great time. I also resumed my meditation, and I have never looked back since.

Perhaps one of the most important ingredients of the Bristol programme is 'having fun'; that is, doing things that make your heart sing, in Lawrence LeShan's memorable phrase. At this time I devoured LeShan's books, and still refer to them frequently. (LeShan, an American psychologist, started work in 1947 on the hypothesis that emotional life history might play a part in the development of cancer: even then this was not a new idea).[3] These books have inspired me to take up counselling myself. I did of course seek counselling, but never found a therapist (apart from those at the Centre) who understood exactly what LeShan was driving at. It didn't seem to matter: all was grist to the mill. I was lucky that my GP understood. My oncologist, however, did not. When I tried to tell her that I thought my cancer was linked with my depression, she dismissed the idea. 'Lots of people get divorced and don't get cancer,' she said, which of course is perfectly true. But it is the *meaning* of the event to the individual, not the event itself, which is important, as many writers have pointed out. I did not find it helpful to have people patronisingly dismiss ideas that psychological factors might have played a part in the onset of my cancer: if *I* wanted to search for meaning and it made sense to *me*, that was what was important to me. The people at Bristol (and indeed my own vicar at home) sought to help me shed guilt, not add to it.

But of course I had plenty of risk factors apart from chronic stress to account for my cancer: early onset of menstruation, late menopause, late childbearing, HRT and a family history of the disease. Perhaps they were all significant. I now had to put them behind me. What the Bristol Centre helped me to do was to use the cancer crisis as an opportunity to move forward, to be released from past hurts and to find new ways of living and, particularly, loving. This meant spending more time relaxing with the family, and we had a number of memorable holidays.

By September 1990 I had co-founded a new cancer support group in my home area and had just embarked on a postgraduate diploma course in counselling. During a trip round Brittany I had come across a book in French on psychology and cancer, and had signed a contract to translate it. I had a full programme of work ahead of me, and did not in the least relish taking on any more; but the publication of the now notorious *Lancet* paper could not be ignored, and I embarked on a campaign to challenge its results, together with Isla Bourke and the other women who joined the Bristol Survey Support Group.

I actually saw the paper before publication. I happened to be in Bristol at the end of August 1990, doing some voluntary work for the Centre. A few of us were entrusted with the confidential information that the dreadful news was about to break. I realised that the paper about to be published was about *me*. I asked to see it. When I read it I was appalled, and immediately wrote a 12-page critique which I would stand by today. I became wary as soon as I read the first page, on which I found the statement: 'In England, however, complementary medicines are not available on prescription.' I knew this to be false: I myself had vitamin and mineral supplements on NHS prescription, and knew others who had been prescribed the mistletoe extract Iscador. If the authors could not get such an elementary fact right, what faith could one have in their research? I read the rest of the paper with growing irritation and alarm. If I had been a junior copy-editor on the *Lancet* I would not have passed it for press.

After it had appeared, I wrote a letter to the *Lancet* which the editor declined to publish. Among other things, I pointed out that no figure was given for the deaths of the controls. To this day, *we do not know how many of the controls died.* Following our later explorations of what went wrong and our correspondence with the *Lancet*, Professor Chilvers said in an unpublished letter to the *Lancet* that the number of deaths among the controls was 100. This cannot be correct, since it is inconsistent with other figures given in the paper. In the words of the *Hospital Doctor* editorial headline of 13 September 1990, 'Slur figures don't add up'. This is just one example of the carelessness that it does not take statistical expertise to notice. But I was glad that my husband, an actuary, was on hand to advise on statistical matters.

The next five years were the busiest of my life. But this time I was not going to let stress get to me: I had my own health to think of. If I couldn't stay well, I was not putting into practice what I had learnt at the Centre. I continued with the routines I had devised for myself: a gentle jog every morning, sensible eating (though I was no longer nearly as strict as I had been the first year after my diagnosis), and as much fun as possible. I completed my counselling training and started working locally. I also translated Guex's *An Introduction to Psycho-oncology*, which led to invitations to conferences in Switzerland. I did voluntary work for several cancer charities – Breast Cancer Care, BACUP, CancerLink, and of course my own cancer support group. I produced a bi-monthly newsletter for the group and several articles for journals. All my skills were being used: writing, translating, speaking, and my newly acquired counselling training. None of this would have happened if I had not had cancer. My life is now so rewarding that I cannot therefore regret having had the disease. I believe my experience has made me more tolerant and more loving, both of myself and other people. It has also enabled me to find strengths that I never knew I had. I have stopped being uncertain of my abilities, afraid of speaking out. When you have once faced death, challenging the heads of the giant cancer charities does not seem very frightening.

I still feel intensely annoyed that the *Lancet* paper has not been withdrawn. I believe it should no longer stand in the medical literature. In June 1995 I heard it being cited at a conference in Switzerland as if it were a valid and respectable piece of work. Luckily I was able to stand up and correct this misapprehension. But until it is withdrawn, such citations will continue. I do not think this should be allowed to happen.

During the last few years I have learnt much about breast cancer and its treatments, and though I was originally willing to accept orthodox therapy, I am not at all sure that this did me much good. After the *Lancet* paper was published I became curious about my original pathology and prognosis, and persuaded the surgeon who had taken over my file from my retired consultant to give me the details. I was not allowed to actually *see* the file, or photocopy the contents, but the surgeon read out to me the salient points. It emerged that I had had a fast-growing, aggressive 5 cm (2 in) tumour (Grade III), with two underarm lymph nodes affected. After surgery (removal of the lump and sampling of the lymph nodes) my treatment consisted of six weeks' radiotherapy followed by two years' prescription of the anti-oestrogen drug tamoxifen.

So was my survival due to this additional medical treatment? Most probably not. Research shows that Grade III tumours do not benefit from tamoxifen.[4] The side effects I suffered included the loss of the top notes of my singing voice. So for me, a person with a keen interest in music and pleasure in singing, the adverse events associated with tamoxifen almost certainly outweighed any hypothetical benefit. The same goes for radiotherapy, which has left me with severe fibrosis (painful hardening of tissue). Although radiotherapy reduces the risk of local recurrence, it confers no long-term survival benefit, according to a recent worldwide overview of 58 trials. The *British Medical Journal* has reported: "'It seems that radiotherapy prevented some breast cancer deaths but caused some other deaths, so we need to find ways of getting the benefits without the risks," said Mr Richard Gray, one of the authors of the review.'[5]

Now, nine years after my original surgery, I am apparently disease-free and very fit. So what have been the additional factors which have helped me to survive without recurrences, in spite of my poor prognosis initially?

When I was first diagnosed my GP said, 'Cancer is a mysterious disease, and we simply don't know how or why people survive. Francis Chichester sailed round the world with lung cancer.' He was prepared to allow that psychological factors could be important. I am sure that in my case they were. Even before I went to Bristol I had begun to make major psychological changes. My work for my brother's sail training project made me look outwards again after my long years of introspection. That was just the beginning. The Cancer Help Centre and the books of Lawrence LeShan further helped me to use the crisis of cancer as a turning point. Ever since then I have been doing the things that really interested me.

The second crisis that hit me with the publication of the *Lancet* report could have been a severe setback, as indeed it was for the Centre itself. I could have done without all the extra work involved in challenging its results, but this too has provided opportunities. Through it I have learnt much about clinical trials and medical research. Willy-nilly I have become an 'activist', which has led to rewarding contacts with other women, not only in Britain but also abroad. At the *Lancet* conference on breast cancer in Brugge in April 1994, one of the poster presentations suggested that 'those who decide to become involved in political advocacy are far less likely to become depressed; this is important because depression is known to have a negative effect on a patient's treatment and hoped-for recovery'.[6]

So in my case I believe that psychological factors, which loomed large in the onset of the disease, also played a major part in its remission. And without a mental readjustment I would not have made changes to my physical way of life: my diet, exercise programme and so on. I still wonder whether simply coming off hormone replacement therapy helped to prevent cancer recurrence: I read recently of a case where a tumour completely disappeared in six weeks after HRT was stopped.[7] Would a 'watch and wait' policy have resolved my problem without surgery? I shall never know.

More important is to find the meaning of life now. 'For the meaning of life differs from man to man, from day to day and from hour to hour', as Victor Frankl expressed it 50 years ago. These words from a survivor of Auschwitz offer a challenge to the survivors of cancer. Frankl goes on:

> As each situation in life represents a challenge to man and presents a problem for him to solve, the question of the meaning of life may actually be reversed. Ultimately, man should not ask what the meaning of his life is, but rather he must recognize that it is *he* who is asked. In a word, each man is questioned by life; and he can only answer to life by *answering for* his own life; to life he can only respond by being responsible.[8]

The imperative that follows is: 'So live as if you were already living for the second time ...', which for me is as apt a maxim as any.

Notes and References

1   Eysenck, H.J. 'Cancer and personality', in Cooper, C.L. and Watson, M. (eds) *Cancer and Stress* 1991; Chichester: Wiley.
2   Hill, A. *In Pursuit of Publishing* 1988; London: John Murray.
3   LeShan, L., *Cancer as a Turning Point* 1989; Bath: Gateway, p. 6.
4   Johnson, A.E., Bennett, M.H., Cheung, C.W.D., Cox, S.J. and Sales, J.E.L., 'The management of individual breast cancers'. *The Breast* 1995; 4: 100–11.
5   Godlee, F. 'Review confirms lumpectomy as safe as mastectomy'. *British Medical Journal* 1995; 311: 1451–2.
6   Balaban, B.J. 'Advocacy in treatment of breast cancer patients'. *The Challenge of Breast Cancer* 1994; Brugge (Lancet conference programme; London: The Lancet Ltd, p. 62).
7   Powles, T.J. and Hickish, T. 'Breast cancer response to hormone replacement therapy withdrawal'. *Lancet* 1995; 345: 1442.
8   Frankl, V.E. *Man's Search for Meaning: an introduction to logotherapy* (first published in Germany in 1946 under the title *Ein Psycholog erlebt das Konzentrationslager*). Revised and enlarged edn. trans. Ilse Lasch, 1987 edn., London: Hodder & Stoughton, pp. 110–11 (trans. first published 1962).

Coda

Heather Goodare

'It is when I am weak that I am strong' — 2 Corinthians 12:10

So can the self affect the course of cancer? Logically, if psychological factors can contribute to the onset of cancer, they can also play a part in recovery. A recent study looked at 33 individuals who have lived for an extended period despite a 'terminal' medical prognosis.[1] The author, Warren Berland, tackles the question of how far retrospective self-reports are accurate: the same question arises with this book. Looking back at my own contribution, I acknowledge freely that I have been selective in my self-report (it would otherwise have been far too long). But I have tried to be honest, and where possible I have checked it against notes made contemporaneously.

Berland also asks 'how can we know whether patients' self-reports have any relation to factors that actually influence healing and survival?' To what extent do patients distort their narratives? I don't think it matters very much if there is distortion: this will inevitably occur. People will select or 'distort' for two main reasons: to preserve privacy or avoid offence, and to attribute meaning to their own experience. (In what way can the opinion of the consultant who sees the patient for a few minutes in each year of follow-up be more 'true' than the patient's own self-report?) I do find it very interesting, though, that Berland's key findings were that 'support of family and friends, and changes in attitude, were the most significant attributions regarding recovery – surpassing even the role of medical treatment, both conventional and alternative.'

We also need to ask to what extent adverse events can affect survival after the onset of illness.[2] The stories here seem to point to a connection in some cases. Sigyn's long struggle to have her disease acknowledged, let alone treated, must have been a serious setback emotionally, as well as saddling her with the huge physical handicap of a very late diagnosis. Those who knew her would not have characterised her as bitter (quite the opposite), but she must have borne much inward stress.

It is important too to try to assess the emotional damage done by the *Lancet* report itself to the women who willingly participated in the study. Among this small sample, Joanna seems to have been the one who was the most deeply affected, perhaps because she had taken the whole Bristol programme so very seriously, especially in her own work as a counsellor. 'I believe the *Lancet* report was a major blow to her' writes her husband, implying that this may have accelerated the disease process.

There may have been others who lost faith in what they were doing; who, while not believing the report, felt perhaps there could not have been smoke without fire. The Centre itself seemed to waver, and made modifications to its programme: the impact on the staff was severe. There was also an impact not just on women who had taken part in the survey, but on other patients who had visited Bristol, especially women with breast cancer. In one case, while the woman herself remained emotionally robust, her teenage daughter became distraught, thinking her mother must be about to die. This girl needed professional counselling before she could regain mental health.[3]

As to whether or not people who go to Bristol are 'different' in some way from the general population of cancer patients, we still have no clear evidence one way or the other. Sir Walter Bodmer, the then director of research at the ICRF, reckoned that a 'useful observation to emerge from the study' was that 'patients are attracted to complementary medicine when they feel their outlook is unpromising'.[4] We surely did not need such a report to tell us anything so obvious. Indeed, some people only seek the help of the Centre on the recurrence of their cancer, or when all else has failed and orthodox doctors have declared 'There is nothing more we can do.'

However, 'disasters can lead to opportunities',[5] and the Bristol study is no exception. The work of the Bristol Survey Support Group has shown that the subjects of research must be respected as more than mere statistics. Indeed, a rich vein of material lies unexploited unless such subjects are truly listened to, and researchers would do well to make better use of them as a resource for designing research that is both more relevant to patients' needs and avoids obvious and preventable pitfalls.[6]

Further than this, we might with profit engage the conscious cooperation of patients right from the start in any research that has a psychosocial component. The major complaints of the women in this survey were not just that the statistics were poor, but that the methods used were inappropriate and that the promised quality of life study was never undertaken. The study of holistic medicine demands holistic research methods. New ways must be found of marrying qualitative and quantitative approaches: both have something to contribute.

Finally, what this book clearly illustrates is that the naïve research subject is a myth. The 'father' of client-centred therapy, Carl Rogers, went further, saying:

Suppose we enlisted every 'subject' as an 'investigator'! Instead of the wise researcher measuring changes in his subjects, suppose he enlisted them all as coresearchers. There is now ample evidence that the so-called naïve subject is a figment of the imagination. The moment a person becomes the object of psychological investigation he starts developing his own fantasies as to the purpose of the study. Then, depending on his temperament and his feeling for the researcher, he sets out either to help develop the finding he thinks is wanted, or to defeat the purpose of the study. Why not bypass all this by making him a member of the research team?[7]

If this had been done in the case of the Bristol study, perhaps some worthwhile findings might have emerged. The anonymous 'controls' whose data were simply culled from cancer registries without their knowledge or consent might also have had something useful to say on the matter.

The women in this survey were distressed at the way in which they were used as pawns[8] in what they saw as a stage battle between orthodox and so-called 'alternative' practitioners. They saw the Bristol Centre not as 'alternative' but as complementary to mainstream medicine, which indeed it has always been. In nearly every case the women went to Bristol to find something not readily available to them locally in National Health Service settings. However, in the past few years the value of complementary approaches in the care of cancer patients has been recognised,[9] and many hospices and cancer centres now offer a range of gentle therapies. This is surely as it should be: as Rachel remarked in our film *Cancer Positive*, 'We should all be working together.'

Notes and References

1   Berland, W. 'Can the self affect the course of cancer? Unexpected cancer recovery: why patients believe they survive'. *Advances* 1995; 11 (4): 5–19.

2   Ramirez, A.J. et al. 'Stress and relapse of breast cancer'. *British Medical Journal* 1989; 298: 291–3.

3   The story was told by Lynda McGilvray in *The Cancer War Story*, BBC 2, 23 May 1995.

4   Bodmer, W. 'Bristol Cancer Help Centre' (letter). *Lancet* 1990 (Nov. 10); 336: 1188.

5   Goodare, H. and Smith, R. 'The rights of patients in research'. *British Medical Journal* 1995; 310: 1277–8.

6   Bradburn, J., Maher, J., Adewuyi-Dalton, R., Grunfeld, E., Lancaster, T. and Mant, D. 'Developing clinical trial protocols: the use of patient focus groups'. *Psycho-oncology* 1995; 4 (2): 107–12.

7   Rogers, C.R. *Encounter Groups* 1973 edn., Harmondsworth: Penguin, p. 167 (first published 1970).

8   Bourke, I. and Goodare, H. 'Bristol Cancer Help Centre' (letter). *Lancet* 1991 (Nov. 30); 338: 1401.

9   Expert Advisory Group on Cancer to the Chief Medical Officers of England and Wales. *A Policy Framework for Commissioning Cancer Services* ('The Calman Report') Department of Health 1995: para 4.2.17.

Appendix I
Request to the Charity Commission from the Bristol Survey Support Group for an Independent Inquiry*

Introduction

We refer to the publication in *The Lancet* dated 8 September 1990 of the interim report 'Survival of patients with breast cancer attending Bristol Cancer Help Centre', by F.S. Bagenal, D.F. Easton, E. Harris, C.E.D. Chilvers, and T.J. McElwain, and its effects on us, a group of women who took part in the survey and whose medical records were used in its preparation.

The report was published amid much media attention, following a leak to the press and a large press conference held at the headquarters of the ICRF. The sensational press release alleged that breast cancer patients attending the Bristol Centre were 'likely to fare worse' compared with controls and that 'some aspect of the Bristol regimen may be the cause'. There followed a series of press articles which caused great distress to Bristol patients in general and to the women who had taken part in the survey in particular. The Bristol Centre itself was badly affected, losing patients, credibility, and funding.

The project was funded by the two major cancer charities, the Imperial Cancer Research Fund (ICRF) and the Cancer Research Campaign (CRC). It was initiated after a visit to the Bristol Centre by a group of medical researchers.

The group included Dr Walter (now Sir Walter) Bodmer, then Director of Research at the Imperial Cancer Research Fund. The

---

* The complete *Request* ran to 282 pages and included a large number of supporting documents (cited as appendices and addenda). So as to avoid unwieldiness, the main text only is reproduced here, with references to the supporting documents deleted.

project is listed in the ICRF Scientific Report 1991 as attached to the Cancer Genetics Laboratory of which he was the Head. Professor T.J. McElwain, the senior author of the report, was also a member of the group: his Chair of Medicine was endowed by the Cancer Research Campaign. The other members were Mrs Clair Chilvers, then of the CRC Section of Epidemiology, Dr Peter Maguire, Director of the CRC Psychological Medicine Group, and Professor Ian McColl.

The research was carried out in the Section of Epidemiology at the Institute of Cancer Research: again, the Chair of Epidemiology is endowed by the CRC, and Dr Galloway (CRC Public Relations Dept) stated in letters to the *Independent* and *Guardian* newspapers that the study 'was carried out by CRC's Epidemiology Department at the ICR'.

We give this background information in order to stress that the charities concerned, ICRF and CRC, did not simply put up the money: *they were closely involved with the planning and execution of the research at all stages.*

After much correspondence in the medical press, the authors admitted in *The Lancet* on 10 November 1990 that the Bristol women were more ill at entry to the study than were the control women. However, this news did not receive nearly as much press coverage as the original article and did not redress the balance. The damage had been done.

Our complaint

The grounds of our complaint are as follows:

1. That the two cancer charities, CRC and ICRF, should have kept a close watching brief on the research, ensuring quality control. This was not done …

2. That the two charities accepted at face value, and without their own independent evaluation and peer-review, the findings of the research team.

3. That they publicised these findings through their press conference in an irresponsible and sensational manner, with a press release that went beyond the paper itself, and contained at least one error of fact.

4. That they did nothing to stop (indeed, they encouraged) premature publication of a speculative interim report, whose findings were entirely inconclusive. We knew at the time that the

research had lasted less than two years: we have recently discovered that the *average* time over which the Bristol cases were observed was six months (unpublished letter from Professor Chilvers to *The Lancet*).

5. That after Sir Walter Bodmer admitted publicly that the research was flawed, the two bodies nevertheless continued to fund it. (The actual period of funding is not clear, but according to Professor Chilvers the work continued until October 1991.)

6. That Sir Walter Bodmer, though disclaiming involvement in the actual work, was nevertheless closely involved from the very beginning with the research design (as mentioned in the protocol [research plan]) ...

7. That even after the report was acknowledged by Sir Walter Bodmer to be flawed, the Scientific Director of the CRC, Professor Gordon McVie, wrote in the *CRC News* an article implying that the findings were valid, and even misrepresenting the facts (i.e., implying that the Bristol women had not had orthodox therapy).

8. That our trust was abused. We gave our consent to the research on the understanding

(a) that it was a five-year study
(b) that it would study quality of life as well as survival.

Neither of these conditions was fulfilled.

Again, we hold the two cancer charities responsible for not ensuring that Dr Peter Maguire (or another) carried out the quality-of-life study as promised in the protocol. At the same time as he was failing to put the Bristol study in hand, CRC was funding him to do other psychological studies of cancer patients: 'Investigation of psychological needs and the development of complementary therapies to help patients ... are becoming a necessary part of cancer care.' (CRC *Annual Report* 1990–91, p. 17.)

9. That we were treated with discourtesy and lack of consideration by the research team, who had asked for our sustained co-operation in filling in annual questionnaires, and then used none of this material in their report. They continued to send us questionnaires after the report was published, with no reference to the results, no explanation, and no apology. CRC's Section of Epidemiology should have given firm ethical guidelines to the staff concerned: they failed to do so.

10. That at the same time that the ICRF were highlighting in their press release for the Bristol survey the possibly 'harmful' effects of the vegetarian, wholefood diet advocated at Bristol, they were planning to support the £2 million EPIC [European Prospective Investigation into Cancer] trial on diet and cancer. The press release for this trial claims that a diet rich in fruit, vegetables and cereals is beneficial.

11. That all these actions were detrimental to the well-being of the cancer patients that these two cancer charities aim to serve. We draw your attention to our more detailed paper, written in September 1991, which elaborates some of these points further ('The Patients' Perspective'), and includes the Protocol for the survey.

Conclusion

To conclude, we wish to state that among our group are 22* women whose records were used and whose co-operation was sought to carry out this survey. We feel that the funds raised by willing volunteers in charity shops, holding coffee mornings and jumble sales, and by bequests (very often from cancer patients) have been tragically misspent in the case of the research in which we were involved.

We cannot absolve the two cancer charities from responsibility for their part in failing to monitor the scientific credibility of the survey, and in publicising its results in a manner that has caused us so much anguish. They cannot deny involvement and at the same time organise a press conference on their own premises, subsequently publishing unscientific, emotive, and partisan comments on the affair.

We cannot point to any improper party-political involvement: this would be irrelevant to the issues. But in the case of this research it seems clear to us that the researchers (followed by the sponsoring charities) allowed their personal views about complementary medicine (which they still persist in calling 'alternative') to cloud their judgement. We can find no other explanation for the fact that they published results which were intrinsically absurd, and in any other context (for example, that of a chemotherapy trial) would have been laughed out of court.

* Another woman joined the group later (cf. p. 6)

The scientific and statistical detail of the report is perhaps outside the remit of yourselves, as Charity Commissioners, to investigate. But we believe you have a duty to ensure that in charities that undertake scientific research, especially research on human subjects, the very highest standards of both science and ethics are maintained. In our opinion and in our experience, the CRC and the ICRF have both fallen far below the standard that the public expects of them.

We therefore ask you to undertake an independent inquiry into all the matters we have brought to your attention. May we suggest that the inquiry be chaired by an independent assessor of sufficient standing in the scientific world to command the respect of all the people involved ...

Summary

The grounds of our complaint are:

1. Use of Funds

We submit that neither the CRC nor the ICRF exercised proper supervision over the application of their funds for charitable purposes. Their funds were not, in our opinion, administered in the manner intended by the donors.

> 'Charities must not allow the proportion of effort and resources which are devoted to persuasion to become greater than that which is devoted directly to meeting its objects.'[1]

In our submission, the CRC and the ICRF used their funds in a manner inappropriate to their charitable objects, and detrimental to a third cancer charity, the Bristol Cancer Help Centre.

2. Administrative Practice

The two cancer charities, CRC and ICRF, who sponsored the study, appear to have proceeded in a muddled, ineffective, and irresponsible manner, with scant regard for the welfare of the

---

1 *Charities: A Framework for the Future*, London, HMSO, May 1989

cancer patients whose interests they are pledged to serve. They have been responsible for poor science and even poorer public relations: we believe that they should be called to account.

2 April 1992

Update of Request to the Charity Commission from the Bristol Survey Support Group 16 November 1992

Introduction

Since our first submission to you of 2 April 1992 we have seen no reason to revise our material. Indeed, subsequent events have only reinforced our position, and provided further evidence of ineffective administration. We have the following additional comments to make.

1. Press release

Sir Walter Bodmer has recently sought to defend this document by reiterating that it used 'only the facts in the Lancet paper'. Two points arise here.

First, though the Lancet paper contained some facts, the press release highlighted not the facts, but the opinions, hypotheses, and highly debatable inferences drawn by the researchers.

Second, the press release went beyond the Lancet paper in the following respects:

(a) *BCHC women 'fare worse'*
The suggestion that women attending the Bristol Centre 'fare worse', with various caveats and possible explanations, came towards the end of the Lancet paper; these words were not used in the abstract at the beginning of the paper, which highlighted two important points: that 85% of BCHC patients were under 55 at diagnosis, and that more than half had experienced recurrence of their disease before entry. The press release, however, said in its *first sentence*:

> 'Women with breast cancer who add to their conventional treatment the alternative therapies offered by the Bristol Cancer Help Centre are *likely to fare worse* compared with controls' (our emphasis).

This immediately draws to the attention of journalists the worst possible conclusions to be drawn from the research, and does not make the important point that the difference between cases and controls 'could be the result of a difference in severity of disease at time of entry to the BCHC, [which] *requires further investigation*' (*Lancet*, our emphasis).

(b) *Younger women*
The Lancet paper stated: '... menopausal status is not a strong prognostic factor for breast cancer'. The press release went beyond this to say, 'previous work has shown that age has no effect on the aggressiveness of the disease', an assertion which cannot be substantiated.

(c) *Statistical analysis*
Three methods of statistical analysis were used: Cox regression, matched, and the landmark method. Only the Cox regression analysis showed a significant difference between the two groups of women.

The researchers made the point that 'In the matched analysis the effect is smaller and non-significant (relapse rate ratio = 1.26, table V) and the landmark method shows little difference between the two groups' (*Lancet*).

And yet the press release said 'Three different forms of statistical analysis were used to try to ensure no bias', the inference being that all three methods had produced the same result, when in fact only *one* (Cox regression) had appeared to show the BCHC women at a disadvantage.

2. Press conference

The claim is made by Sir Walter Bodmer that 'it is standard practice for both the CRC and ICRF to hold a press conference because it is the most practical method for dealing with an inevitable deluge of press queries'. This assumes that the medical correspondents would have featured the *Lancet* article in similar terms even if there had not been a press conference. This is very unlikely, particularly since the statement to the press did not accurately reflect, in content and in balance, the statement in *The Lancet* itself.

The press conference actually had the result that the news (preceded by a 'leak' in the *Sunday Correspondent*) broke two days before *The Lancet* was published, when the paper was not available for informed comment outside the ranks of journalists. Indeed, Alan Massam wrote in the *Evening Standard* (5 September 1990), 'Publication of the Lancet report is believed to have been brought forward at the request of two of Britain's cancer charities because two BBC programmes about the centre are to be screened this month.' This indicates clearly that the CRC and the ICRF were very closely involved indeed in the effort to ensure *maximum publicity* for the report, even at this provisional and interim stage, and as [the journalist] Jeremy Laurance also noted, to pre-empt the television programmes ('Blow to cancer hopes').

We also find it surprising that Professor Karol Sikora was absent from the press conference. Of all people he should have been able to shed some light on the very curious results, as the senior oncologist who above all others knew from his joint project with the Bristol Centre at the Hammersmith Hospital exactly what the 'Bristol' therapies involved (see *Sunday Correspondent*). If the charities had been concerned to put forward a balanced view of the research, then it was surely essential to include a contribution from Professor Sikora. Was he invited?

3. 'Four legs good, two legs bad'

An extraordinary example of the kind of 'doublethink' satirised by Orwell has recently arisen in this area of research. The Cancer Research Campaign is sponsoring a new project at Aberdeen University which 'aims to combat the damaging effect of stress on the body's own ability to fight cancer' with a 'new relaxation therapy'. It turns out that this 'imaginative and innovative' approach is exactly the same type of relaxation therapy that has been pioneered in the UK by the Bristol Cancer Help Centre for the last ten years (and is also used by many cancer patients in local support groups up and down the country as a matter of routine). The CRC can hardly be unaware of this, since they refer to it in their own press release of 7 September 1990.

4. Recognition of error in study design

Sir Walter Bodmer now says that the 'mistake in the study design' (i.e. the women attending Bristol were more ill than the women with whom they were being compared) meant that 'the result would have been the same if the project had run for five years instead of three'. This mistake was acknowledged by Sir Walter himself in a letter to *The Lancet* (10 November 1990). *If this fundamental methodological error was by then irretrievable, why did the two charities continue to support the project instead of cancelling it forthwith?*

Also, why were the researchers allowed to continue to send out questionnaires to women, and even to attempt to persuade them not to withdraw from the project? [A letter appended] clearly shows that the researchers were still (February 1991) denying the basic flaws in their work, and expecting to carry on for a further two years. Their muddled thinking is amply illustrated in this document.

The Editor of *The Lancet*, however, *did* take immediate steps in November 1990 to revise the journal's statistical review procedures.

5. Publicity for amended results

The part played by the ICRF in rectifying matters to the press amounted to a 14-line letter to *The Lancet* (10th November 1990). They held no press conference, and as noted before, the CRC continued to imply that the findings were valid ... And as late as 6 July 1991 Jeremy Laurance, the journalist who first 'leaked' the story in the *Sunday Correspondent*, wrote in *The Telegraph* about 'last year's damaging report on the Bristol Cancer Help Centre, which *showed that* breast cancer patients who supplemented conventional treatment with alternative therapy died sooner than those who stuck to conventional treatment' (our emphasis). We therefore consider that the ICRF's 'best' efforts to make the 'error plain to journalists' were not good enough.

We estimate that 167 column inches were devoted on 6 September 1990 in the national daily press to the initial reports of the alleged *adverse* effects of the Bristol programme. In addition there was a televised press conference, many feature articles were written, and two highly tendentious television programmes were broadcast. The amended report achieved only 72 column inches on 9 November 1990, with little or no coverage in the mass-circulation papers. And this was as a result of BCHC's own press conference; none was held by the cancer charities.

6. Patients' efforts

It was only, we believe, in response to our own efforts as a group of patients affected by the research that the project was finally terminated. Some of the problems we encountered were ably described by the Editor of the *Bulletin of Medical Ethics*.

7. Responsibility

Both charities have repeatedly disowned responsibility for the actual research itself, and yet the close links between the CRC and the ICR in particular are undeniable. The BSSG's letter to the ICR of 30 April 1991 was replied to by the CRC. Clearly Professor Garland *did not regard the matter as his responsibility.* As Professor Garland and Professor McVie say in a letter to the *Observer* of 8 November 1992, 'the Cancer Research Campaign and the Institute of Cancer Research have collaborated successfully over many years and intend to continue'.

To sum up, it is significant, we think, that the press release of September 1990 says 'The two charities decided to *do* the study ...' (our emphasis). Their close involvement and their responsibility at all stages is clear.

8. Conclusions

To conclude, we request that we be given an opportunity to make positive recommendations for the future conduct of research on patients, whether funded or actually carried out by these two powerful cancer charities. It is clear that the guidelines given by the Royal College of Physicians were not followed in the research in which we were involved. We draw your attention in particular to the following paragraph:

> In studies which involve any sustained cooperation on the part of the patient it is good practice to make arrangements to inform participants of the outcome of the research in broad terms and to combine this with a letter of thanks. (Royal College of Physicians, *Research involving patients*, 1990, para 9.2)

If this basic courtesy had been observed, premature publication of erroneous results might well have been avoided.

But we would go further than this, and declare that the interests of patients are not served by the polarisation of the two sides of medicine, orthodox and complementary: we should like to see them working together, using a genuinely holistic approach. The patient should not be the battle-ground for gladiatorial combat such as we witnessed at the time of the ICRF/CRC press conference. As 'consumers' of medicine we should like to see co-operation and cordiality between medical practitioners of all kinds, and we look forward to the day when every district general hospital offers complementary therapies to people with cancer.

Appendix II
Findings of Inquiry under Section 8 Charities Act 1993
1. Cancer Research Campaign
2. Imperial Cancer Research Fund
[Extracts]

The Inquiry was established following a request that the Commissioners consider the conduct of the Cancer Research Campaign (CRC) and Imperial Cancer Research Fund (ICRF) in connection with the funding of a study into the survival rate of patients attending the Bristol Cancer Help Centre (the Bristol Study).

As a result of the Inquiry it has been found that although the arrangements by the two charities met a number of the requirements for the funding of research by charities, their procedures for the supervision of research and control of the research results were not entirely satisfactory so that the charities could not be certain that charity funds awarded to independent researchers were properly applied ...

The Inquiry found that no one adequately supervised the Bristol Study ... Although the funding charities acted in accordance with their usual procedures, the charities neither supervised the research themselves nor arranged, through written agreements, for an agent to supervise the work on their behalf. The Institute of Cancer Research, which employed the lead researcher, did not consider it had any responsibility to supervise the work.

In acting in this way the CRC and ICRF could not ensure that the charitable funds were properly applied either by exercising, or by arranging for, any supervision of the research. Nor was it able to control the procedures followed. In this respect the trustees of the CRC and ICRF did not discharge their duties as trustees of the charitable funds involved …

The CRC and ICRF said that they followed their usual practice in not reviewing themselves, or ensuring the review of, the results of the Bristol study prior to any publication … In not ensuring that the results of the study were evaluated prior to publication the trustees of the CRC and ICRF could not fulfil their duty of ensuring that the research had been properly and adequately carried out …

The Commissioners note that the ICRF did evaluate the results quickly after their publication. Shortly after the results were published, following immediate concerns about the findings, Sir Walter Bodmer, Director of Research of the ICRF, wrote a letter to the Lancet stating that:

"Our own evaluation is that the study's results can be explained by the fact that women going to Bristol had more severe disease than control women."

Charity Commission, London, 6 January 1994

Appendix III
Chronological List of Events

23 March 1983	Studio discussion of BBC series *A Gentle Way with Cancer*. Participants included Dr Walter Bodmer, Professor Tim McElwain and Professor Ian McColl.
1985	Research plan (Protocol) approved by the Royal Marsden Hospital Research Ethics Committee.
June 1986	First patients recruited into study at Bristol.
May 1987	Protocol approved by the Research Ethics Committee at Crawley Hospital, which provided a proportion of the controls.
Oct. 1987	Last patients recruited into study at Bristol.
July 1990	Paper received at the Bristol Cancer Help Centre.
2 Sept. 1990	First press 'leak'.
5 Sept. 1990	Press conference at ICRF headquarters.
8 Sept. 1990	Paper published in the *Lancet*.
13/14 Sept. 1990	BBC 2 programmes *The Cancer Question*, featuring the 'Bristol study'.
10 Nov. 1990	Flaws acknowledged by research team in letter to the *Lancet*.
26 Nov. 1990	Suicide of Professor Tim McElwain.
Jan. 1991	Formation of Bristol Survey Support Group
Oct. 1991	Research project terminated
Nov. 1991	Publication of letter from BSSG in the *Lancet*
2 Apr. 1992	Channel 4 television programme *Cancer Positive* in the series *Free for All*
6 Jan. 1994	Publication of Charity Commission Report 'Findings of Inquiry under Section 8 Charities Act 1993: 1. Cancer Research Campaign. 2. Imperial Cancer Research Fund.

21 Jan. 1994	Discussion on Radio 4's *Woman's Hour* between Professor Nick Wright (ICRF), Dr Richard Nicholson (*Bulletin of Medical Ethics*) and Heather Goodare (BSSG).
26 Feb. 1994	Publication of letter from BSSG in *British Medical Journal*
23 May 1995	Broadcast of film *The Cancer War Story* in the series *Taking Liberties*, BBC 2
14 June 1995	House of Commons Debate of Early Day Motion no. 1203, proposed by Jean Corston MP

EXAMPLE OF QUESTIONNAIRE SENT TO PATIENTS IN THE 'BRISTOL STUDY'

Quest2
24.11.87

Date 28 Jan '88

Name _____   Serial No. | | | | | |
                                              13.01.87.

Could we ask you to complete this short questionnaire to give us some details of your health and treatments during the past year.

1. Are you having any of the following medical treatments at the present time? Please tick all boxes that apply to you.

Radiotherapy |_| chemotherapy |_| hormone therapy |✓| none |_| other |_|
                                    (e.g. tamoxifen)

    If other please specify _____ none _____

2. Are you having any of the following treatments at the present time?

    Yes |✓| No |✗|

    How often do you use them?   (approximately)

	(1) Never	(2) 3 Monthly	(3) Monthly	(4) Weekly	(5) More than once weekly	(6) Daily	(7) More than once daily
Acupuncture							
Homeopathy							
Herbal Remedies							
Iscador							
Other treatment			approx ✓				

If other, please specify type of treatment Aromatherapy : e.g. massage of breast which has become slightly swollen as a result of radiation.

3. Which of the following is included in your diet at the moment?

    Vegetables   Yes |✓| No |_| Fish   Yes |✓| No |_|
    Dairy products Yes |✓| No |_| Meat   Yes |_| No |✓|
    Free-range Eggs Yes |✓| No |_| No red meat: poultry occasionally

I follow a largely vegetarian diet. any lapses are for social rather than ideological reasons! Amounts of dairy produce, eggs & fish strictly limited.

4. Do you use any of the following therapies at present?

Yes |✓| No |☐|

And how often?

	(1) Never	(2) 3 Monthly	(3) Monthly	(4) Weekly	(5) More than once weekly	(6) Daily	(7) More than once daily
Imaging				✓			
Counselling			✓				
Diet						✓	
Biofeedback (only at Bristol)		✓					
Healing				✓			
Meditation						✓	
Other: exercise including Yoga				✓		✓	

If other, please specify type of therapy:

I have taken up Yoga, which I regard as helpful therapy: the exercises are just what I need a year after my radiotherapy to stretch the muscles gently. (weekly classes)

5. Do you take any of the following supplements to your diet?

Yes |✓| No |☐|

―If yes, please tick any boxes that apply to you.

Vit B |✓| Selenium |✓| Beta-carotene |✓|
Vit C |✓| Herbal mixture |☐| Zinc |✓|
Vit D |☐| Evening Primrose Oil |☐| Other |☐|
Vit E |✓| Carrot juice |☐|

6. Does your G.P. know you have attended or are attending the Bristol Cancer Help Centre?

Yes |✓| No |☐|

7. To what extent is your G.P. supportive of the approach to cancer encouraged by the Bristol Cancer Help Centre.

Very supportive |✓| Rather lacking in support |☐|

Fairly supportive |☐| In total disagreement |☐|

Makes no comment |☐|

My GP prescribes all my vitamin and mineral supplements on the NHS.

8. Does your consultant know you have attended or are attending the Bristol Cancer Help Centre?

Yes |✓| No |☐|

9. To what extent is your consultant supportive of the approach to cancer encouraged by the Bristol Cancer Help Centre.

Very supportive	|☐|	Rather lacking in support	|✓|
Fairly supportive	|☐|	In total disagreement	|☐|
Makes no comment	|☐|		

10. Since going to the Bristol Centre, are you coping with your illness:

A great deal better |✓| (NB The root illness was not Cancer
                                but depression!)

A little better |☐|

About the same |☐|

A little worse |☐|

Much worse |☐|

11. Date of last visit to the Bristol Cancer Help Centre   7.1.88

If you would like to say more about your life since going to the Bristol Cancer Help Centre please use this space.

Since going to the B.C.H.C. my life has been transformed. I had suffered from depression for years but had recovered shortly before cancer was diagnosed. Nevertheless major changes still needed to be made to my lifestyle, and this was made possible by my visit to Bristol (together with my husband). I have started working again almost full time and am now a member of a local Cancer Self-help group, feeling confident enough to help other patients who are worse off than me.

PTO

The meditation taught at Bristol was for me the hardest part of the programme to follow at first, but is now the most important. It has led me back to the Christian mystics and has enriched my life immeasurably, besides helping me to concentrate (essential in my work as an editor). I have been far more healthy generally during the past year than during the previous ten, with no colds to speak of. My husband and I went on a very energetic cycling holiday in the summer, which I much enjoyed.

Apart from the Bristol Centre, I have found Bacup, ~~and~~ New Approaches to Cancer and Cancerlink useful as suppliers of resource material: the great thing that they do at Bristol is to encourage you to help yourself. Bacup sent me a helpful booklet on lymphodema with exercises to follow. (My consultant has not raised the matter of exercise, though I did check with her that my proposed programme was OK.)

14/2/88

Select Bibliography

1. The Bristol Study

Immediately preceding publication of the *Lancet* paper, on 6 September 1990, there were 167 column inches of comment on it in the national daily press alone, followed by many letters. The following selected list features mainly the longer, more serious articles, and books referring to the study. The interested reader should also, of course, look up the letters immediately following publication of the paper in the *Lancet* itself, in September–November 1990 (see Bhopal and Tonks, below).

Batt, S., *Patient No More: the politics of breast cancer*, London, Scarlet Press, 1995.

Bennet, G., 'Bristol Cancer Help Centre' (letter), *Lancet* vol. 336, 22 September 1990, p. 744.

Bhopal, R.S. and Tonks, A., 'The role of letters in reviewing research', *British Medical Journal* vol. 38, 18 June 1994, pp. 1582–3.

Bodmer, W., 'Bristol Cancer Help Centre' (letter), *Lancet* vol. 336, 10 November 1990, p. 1188.

Boulter, P.S., 'Bristol Cancer Help Centre' (letter), *Lancet* vol. 336, 22 September 1990, p. 744.

Bourke, I., 'Patient power', *Network* (Breast Cancer Care newsletter), Spring 1994, p. 3.

Bourke, I. and Goodare, H., 'Bristol Cancer Help Centre' (letter) *Lancet* vol. 338, November 1991, p. 1401.

Bourke, I. and Goodare, H., 'Free for All: "Cancer positive"' (letter), *British Medical Journal* vol. 304, 30 May 1992, p. 1445.

Daniel, R., 'The Bristol Cancer Help Centre: surviving and growing through our crisis', *Holistic Health* Summer 1991, pp. 5–6.

Dean, M., 'London Perspective: Cancer, *The Lancet*, and the media', *Lancet* vol. 336, 22 September 1990, pp. 737–8.

Faulder, C., *Always a Woman: a practical guide to living with breast surgery*, London, Thorsons, 1992.

Forbes, A., 'Raising the will to live', *Here's Health* January 1991, pp. 8–9.

Goodare, H., 'The Bristol Cancer Research: a patient's view', *Self and Society: the European Journal of Humanistic Psychology* vol. XIX no. 3, 1991, pp. 37–40.

Goodare, H., 'Charity Commission upholds BSSG complaint', *Centrepiece* (BCHC newsletter) no. 17, January/February 1994, p. 1.

Goodare, H., 'Wrong results should be withdrawn' (letter) *British Medical Journal* vol. 308, 26 February 1994, p. 593.

Goodare, H., 'Counseling people with cancer: questions and possibilities', *Advances: the journal of mind-body health* vol. 10, no. 2, Spring 1994, pp. 4–17.

Goodare, H., 'Charities in search of medical advice', *The Times Higher Education Supplement* 30 September 1994.

Goodare, H. and Smith, R., 'The rights of patients in research', *British Medical Journal* vol. 310, no. 6990, 1995, pp. 1277–8.

Goodare, K.J. 'Bristol Cancer Help Centre' (letter) *Lancet* vol. 340, 25 July 1992, p. 248.

Hayes, R.J., Smith, P.G., Carpenter, L., 'Bristol Cancer Help Centre' (letter), *Lancet* vol. 336, 10 November 1990, p. 1185.

Heyse-Moore, L., 'Bristol Cancer Help Centre' (letter), *Lancet* vol. 336, 22 September 1990, p. 743.

Hodgkinson, L. and Metcalfe, J., *The Bristol Experience*, London, Vermilion, 1995 (see especially chapter 3).

Horton, R., 'Revising the research record', *Lancet* vol. 346, 16 December 1995, pp. 1610–11.

Hunt, L., 'News of death greatly exaggerated', *Independent*, 15 November 1993, p. 19.

Hunt, L., 'Cancer charities attacked for lack of fund control', *Independent*, 7 January 1994, p. 5.

James, N., Reed, A., 'Bristol Cancer Help Centre' (letter), *Lancet* vol. 336, 22 September 1990, p. 744.

Johnson, A.E., 'Growth rates of breast tumours' (letter), *Lancet* vol. 339, 4 January 1992, p. 59.

Lewith, G., 'Bristol Cancer Help Centre' (letter), *Lancet* vol. 336, 22 September 1990, p. 744.

Lloyd, A., 'Rebuilding the centre', *Nursing Times* vol. 88, no. 26, 24 June 1992, pp. 16–17.

Lorch, J., Macwhinnie, I., Christie-Smith, H. and Stacey, M., 'The Bristol Cancer Help Centre Research Study', *Caduceus* no. 12, Autumn/Winter 1990/91, pp. 4–10.

Merritt, J., 'Hope outside the cancer ward', *Observer* 14 July 1991, pp. 49–50.

Metcalfe, J., 'Gentle cancer care: where does it go from here?', *Journal of Alternative & Complementary Medicine*, February 1991, pp. 24–5.

Monro, J., Payne, M., 'Bristol Cancer Help Centre' (letter), *Lancet* vol. 336, 22 September 1990, pp. 743–4.

Nicholson, R., Editorial and news article, 'Bristol study should be retracted', *Bulletin of Medical Ethics* December 1991, pp. 1, 3–6.

Nicholson, R., Editorial and news article, 'Charity Commission criticizes medical research charities', *Bulletin of Medical Ethics* December 1993, pp. 1, 6.

Nicholson, R., News article, 'Bristol study continues to cause debate', *Bulletin of Medical Ethics* May 1995, pp. 3–5.

Pfeffer, N., 'Cancer research and ethics: report of the CERES autumn open meeting', *Ceres News* no. 8, Autumn/Winter 1991, London, Consumers for Ethics in Research, pp. 4–8.

Popay, J. and Williams, G. (eds) *Researching the People's Health*, London, Routledge, 1994 (see chapter 5: 'The power of lay knowledge' by Meg Stacey).

Potterton, D., 'Hook, line and sinker', *Therapy Weekly* 7 March 1991, p. 6.

Rawlins, I., 'Vital statistics', *Health Service Journal* 17 February 1994, p. 35.

Read, C., *Preventing Breast Cancer: the politics of an epidemic*, London, Pandora, 1995.

Richards, T., 'Death from complementary medicine', *BMJ* vol. 301, 15 September 1990, pp. 510–11.

Roberts, H. (ed.), *Women's Health Matters*, London, Routledge, 1992.

Sheard, T.A.B., 'Bristol Cancer Help Centre', (letters), *Lancet* vol. 336, 15 September 1990, p. 683; 10 November 1990, pp. 1185–6.

Smith, R., 'Charity Commission censures British cancer charities', *British Medical Journal* vol. 308, 1994, pp. 155–6.

Stacey, M., 'Bristol Cancer Help Centre', *Holistic Health* Winter 1991, p. 29.

Tobias, J., 'Surely a natural cancer remedy can't be dangerous – can it?' *British Medical Journal* vol. 301, 22 September 1990, p. 613.

Tobias, J., Baum, M. 'Bristol Cancer Help Centre' (letter), *Lancet* vol. 336, 24 November 1990, p. 1323.

Tonkin, R. and Tee, D., 'Bristol Cancer Help Centre' (letter), *Lancet* vol. 336, 22 September 1990, p. 744.

Walker, M.J., *Dirty Medicine*, London, Slingshot, 1993.

Wetzler, M., 'Surely a natural cancer remedy can't be dangerous' (letters), *British Medical Journal* vol. 301, 20 October 1990, p. 929; 1 December 1990, p. 1280.

Wright, S. 'Bristol Cancer Help Centre' (letter), *Lancet* vol. 336, 22 September 1990, p. 743.

Wright, S.J., 'The Lancet Bristol Cancer Help Centre Study: barrier or stimulus to further research into complementary medicine', *Holistic Medicine* vol. 5, no. 3/4, September/December 1990, pp. 171–5.

2. The holistic approach to cancer

Barasch, M.I., *The Healing Path*, London, Penguin/Arkana, 1995.

Bishop, B., *A Time to Heal*, London, New English Library edn. 1989 (first published 1985).

Borysenko, J. and Borysenko, M. *The Power of the Mind to Heal*, Enfield, Middx, Eden Grove, 1995.

British Medical Association, *Complementary Medicine: new approaches to good practice*, Oxford, Oxford University Press, 1993.

Brohn, P., *Gentle Giants*, London, Century, 1986.

Brohn, P., *The Bristol Programme*, London, Century, 1987.

Charles, R., *Mind, Body and Immunity*, London, Methuen, 1990.

Charles, R., *Food for Healing*, London, Cedar, 1995.

Chopra, D., *Quantum Healing: exploring the frontiers of mind/body medicine*, New York, Bantam, 1989.

Cooper, C.L., Cooper, R.D., and Eaker, L.H., *Living with stress*, Harmondsworth, Penguin, 1988.

Daniel. R. and Goodman, S., *Cancer and Nutrition: the positive scientific evidence*, Bristol, Cancer Help Centre, 1994.

Fink, J.M., *Third Opinion: an international directory to alternative therapy centers for the treatment and prevention of cancer and other degenerative diseases*, New York, Avery, 1992.

Fulder, S. *The Handbook of Complementary Medicine*, 2nd edn., London, Coronet, 1989.

Gawain, S., *Creative Visualization*, London, Bantam, 1980.

Gawler, G., *Women of Silence: the emotional healing of breast cancer*, Melbourne, Hill of Content, 1994.

Gawler, I., *You Can Conquer Cancer*, Melbourne, Hill of Content, 1984.

Gerson, M. *A Cancer Therapy: results of fifty cases*, 5th edn, Bonita, Calif., Gerson Institute, 1990 (first published 1958).

Guex, P., *Introduction to Psycho-oncology*, trans. H. Goodare, London, Routledge, 1993.

Harrison, S., *New Approaches to Cancer*, London, Century, 1987.

Hay, L., *You Can Heal your Life*, London, Eden Grove, 1988.

Hirshberg, C. and Barasch, M.I., *Remarkable Recovery: what extraordinary healings can teach us about getting well and staying well*, London, Headline, 1995.

Kfir, N. and Slevin, M., *Challenging Cancer: from chaos to control*, London, Tavistock/Routledge, 1991.

Kidman, B., *A Gentle Way with Cancer*, London, Century, 1983.

Kübler-Ross, E., *To Live until we Say Good-bye*, Englewood Cliffs, NJ, Prentice-Hall, 1978.

Kübler-Ross, E., *On Death and Dying*, London, Tavistock/Routledge, 1989.

LeShan, L., *You Can Fight for your Life: emotional factors in the treatment of cancer*, Wellingborough, Thorsons, 1984.

LeShan, L., *Cancer as a Turning Point*, Bath, Gateway, 1989.

LeShan, L., *How to Meditate*, Wellingborough, Thorsons, 1989.

Love, S.M., *Dr Susan Love's Breast Book* 2nd edn., New York, Addison Wesley, 1995.

Manning, M., *Matthew Manning's Guide to Self-healing*, Wellingborough, Thorsons, 1989.

Moyers, B., *Healing and the Mind*, London, Aquarian/Thorsons, 1995.

Rippon, S., *The Bristol Recipe Book*, London, Century, 1987.

Siegel, B., *Love, Medicine and Miracles*, London, Arrow, 1988.

Siegel, B., *Peace, Love and Healing*, London, Arrow, 1991.

Siegel, B., *Living, Loving and Healing*, London, Aquarian, 1993.

Simonton, O.C., Matthews-Simonton, S. and Creighton, J.L., *Getting Well Again*, London, Bantam, 1980.

Slevin, M. and Short, R., *Cancer and the Mind: proceedings of an international conference*, London, Mark Allen, 1990.

Spiegel, D., *Living beyond limits: new hope and help for facing life-threatening illness*, New York, Random House, 1993.

Thomas, H. and Sikora, K., *Cancer: a positive approach*, London, Thorsons, 1995.

Thomson, R., *Loving Medicine*, Bath, Gateway, 1989.

Wilber, K. *Grace and Grit*, Dublin, Gill & Macmillan, 1991.

Weiner, M.A., *Maximum Immunity*, Bath, Gateway, 1986.

Wittman, J., *Breast Cancer Journal*, Golden, Colo., Fulcrum, 1993.

Useful Addresses

Action against Breast Cancer
Fairview, Long Wittenham, Oxon OX14 4QJ
Tel: 01865–407384

Breast Cancer Care
Kiln House, 210 New Kings Road, London SW6 4NZ
Tel. nos: Helpline 0171–384 2344
Scotland 0141–353 1050
Freeline 0500–245 345
Administration 0171–384 2984

British Association for Counselling
37A Sheep Street, Rugby, Warwicks CV21 3BX
Tel. 01788–578328

Bristol Cancer Help Centre
Grove House, Cornwallis Grove, Clifton, Bristol BS8 4PG
Tel. nos: Patients' helpline 0117–980 9505
Administration 0117–980 9500
Fundraising 0117–980 9510
Marketing and PR 0117–980 9515

British Association of Cancer United Patients (BACUP)
3 Bath Place, Rivington Street, London EC2A 3JR
Tel. nos: Information 0800–181199 (freephone)
London callers 0171–613 2121
Scotland 0141–553 1553
Counselling service 0171–696 9000
Administration 0171–696 9003

Cancer Relief Macmillan Fund
Anchor House, 15/19 Britten Street, London SW3 3TZ
Tel: 0171–351 7811

CancerLink
17 Britannia Street, London WC1X 9JN
Tel. nos: Information 0171–833 2451
Freephone MAC Helpline for young people 0800–591028
Asian information line (Hindi, Bengali) 0171–713 7867
Administration, groups, supporters 0171–833 2818

Carers National Association
2025 Glasshouse Yard, London EC1A 4JS
Tel. 0171–490 8898

Debra Stappard Cancer Trust
Chapel Farm, Westhumble, Dorking, Surrey RH5 6AY
Tel. 01306–882865

Matthew Manning Healing Centre
39 Abbeygate Street, Bury St Edmunds, Suffolk
Tel. 01284–830222

National Cancer Alliance
33 Aston Street, Oxford OX4 1EW
Tel. 01865–793566

New Approaches to Cancer
5 Larksfield, Englefield Green, Egham, Surrey TW20 0RB
Tel: 01784–433610

Research Council for Complementary Medicine
60 Great Ormond Street, London WC1 3JF
Tel. 0171–833 8897

Royal London Homoeopathic Hospital NHS Trust
Great Ormond Street, London WC1N 3HR
Tel. 0171–833 7276

UK National Breast Cancer Coalition
P.O. Box 8554, London SW8 2ZB
Tel: 0171–720 0945

Index